By Gretchen Craig

NOVELS

Always & Forever: A Saga of Slavery and Deliverance
(The Plantation Series, Book I)
Ever My Love: A Saga of Slavery and Deliverance
(The Plantation Series, Book II)
Evermore: A Saga of Slavery and Deliverance
(The Plantation Series, Book III)

Tansy
Crimson Sky
Theena's Landing

SHORT STORY COLLECTIONS

The Color of the Rose
Bayou Stories: Tales of Troubled Souls
Lookin' for Luv: Five Short Stories

The Lion's Teeth

Gretchen Craig

Pendleton
Press

Published by Pendleton Press.
Copyright © 2015 by Gretchen Craig
www.GretchenCraig.com

Kindle e-book edition available from Amazon.com.

ISBN-13:978-0692427705
ISBN-10: 0692427708

The Lion's Teeth

Chapter One

December, 1810

The Andry plantation,
forty miles north of New Orleans

Charles sat astride his horse surveying the men in his crew, making sure everyone stayed alert, paid attention. Nobody got hurt that way.

Sounded like a thousand bees humming as two of his men dragged a saw blade through the trunk of an ancient cypress. Charles gauged the likely fall when the men made their final cut. A tree that big was going to sound like the end of the world when it hit the ground. He checked again to be sure everyone – the men with the barrels of chain, the ones with the hooks and rope, the men with the wagons and oxen – everyone was out of the way of that trunk about to crash down.

These men were his best team, all of them past their first youth, their backs and arms strengthened by a few years in the cane fields. Most of them were black as men can be, but a couple showed they had a white daddy or granddaddy, their skins, like his own, brown instead of black.

Dark or light, Charles and all of these men shared an African heritage, and all of them belonged to Manuel Andry. Charles, however, had nothing else in common with the other slaves. Those men knew each other, worked side by side day in and day out. They called out good-natured insults and laughed together. Like brothers. Charles was excluded from that. He rode a horse. He had a pair of boots, a felt hat. And secrets.

Charles eyed George steadying the oxen. He was a good man, worked hard. Had three meals a day, a roof over his head, a woman and a few children. If George suspected what was coming and told Andry, he'd get himself a bigger ration of meal and pork for those kids. Maybe a bigger cabin. So Charles kept an eye on George, and on all the others.

Charles's eyes darted to the tell-tale triangular wake rippling the dark water. He slid out of the saddle quick as a snake and strode across the muddy ground. Then the men in the water saw it, too. Charles ignored the hollering and splashing as they rushed to shore. He released the whip from his belt in one smooth motion, raised his arm and flicked his wrist.

The leather whooshed through the air, cracked, and lashed across the head of a twelve foot gator.

The monster bellowed and roiled and thrashed. Its great tail beat at the water, blood from its torn eyes pinking the froth. The smell of stirred-up muck rose from the water as the terrible teeth flashed and snapped at the bloody spray.

Charles snapped the whip again, opening the hide across the creature's snout. It rolled, then retreated beneath the blood-stained foam.

Shaken, Charles clenched his teeth. If that monster had latched onto a man's leg . . .

In the sudden silence, Charles felt their eyes on him. They'd be thinking about the whip, remembering other times they'd heard it crack. He'd held back, always, when he'd had to use it. But they wouldn't know that. At least this time, the flesh it opened was not human. Maybe they'd think that too.

"Where are those damned boys?" He scanned the faces, some slack-jawed, still staring at the swamp water, to settle on the two youngsters who should have been keeping watch for snakes and gators. They shifted their feet and looked at the muddy ground. They knew they'd messed up, playing instead of doing their jobs. Charles made the whip twitch as his eyes burned into them each in turn. When he thought they were as scared as they could get, he cracked the whip loud as he could and snapped it at the dirt in front of the oldest boy's foot.

"You boys got a job to do," he said. "Do it."

George took over from there, separated the boys, scolded them and slapped their backsides.

Charles remounted his horse and stayed until the tree fell, precisely where he'd cleared the ground for it, then left it to George to get the log out of the water.

He took his time riding back to the fields. This time of year, no cauldrons of boiling molasses scented the air. Instead, the heady smell of damp black earth rose from the ground. He tipped his head up to feel the December sun on his face and closed his eyes. He didn't stop often enough to take pleasure in the earth, in the air, in being alive. At the cry of a red-tailed hawk, he opened his eyes and watched the bird's silhouette cross the blue sky.

Alone like this, the muscles in his face relaxed, his shoulders loosened. No one to see, he let himself just be. It wouldn't be long now, he'd end this life as Andry's slave. He would be free, or he would die. But today, he lived, and the sun felt good.

The swamp behind him, he rode through the leafless peach orchard and on to the fields where he had people laying out furrows for the next planting. It was easy work in December compared to the exhausting toil of harvesting the cane and getting it boiled down into sugar. God knew they all needed a spell to catch their breaths, to heal the inevitable bruises and cuts suffered in the rush to get the cane in before the first frost.

He turned into the lane and saw Gilbert Andry and his young cousin on horseback, a group of slaves gathered in front of them. Charles gritted his teeth. Any time he found the master's son near the slaves, there was trouble.

His impulse was to spur his horse on, to break it up before Gilbert committed some new cruelty, but any haste on his part would only add to the excitement.

Charles stopped six feet from Gilbert and the cousin, Mr. Edmund. Leaning on his pommel, he noted Gilbert's fine mount, the roan's coat glowing in the soft winter sun. Gilbert wore his intricately tooled Spanish boots and a fine ruffled shirt. A little short and thick in the thigh, like his daddy, but Gilbert was the ladies' darling with his sun-streaked hair and fair skin. Likely the ladies had never seen him like this, well into his meanness, when his eyes were flat, shallow pools of evil.

Charles kept his voice calm, disinterested. "Morning, Mr. Gilbert."

"Watch this," Gilbert said, grinning. "Pull her elbows behind her," he told Old Gus, a wizened old slave who stood behind Celine.

3

The buttons popped open across her big belly and swollen breasts, baring her from neck to crotch, giving the men a fine view of a woman maybe seven months along.

Malicious glee on his face, Gilbert pointed at her. "Look at those titties. Sticking out, big as melons."

"She done something?"

"Gave me one of those looks. Like she got a demon inside peeping out through those eyes." Gilbert fastened his gaze on Celine's exposed belly. "You think that's a demon baby she's carrying, Edmund?"

Charles eyed the boy, dressed even fancier than his cousin in buff pantaloons, lace at his cuffs, velvet at his collar. Edmund was just a scrawny kid, maybe twelve. Looked like a mite on top of his big gray mare, but here he was, learning how to be a man from Cousin Gilbert. Was he made from the same mold? The kid couldn't take his eyes off Celine's tits, but, Charles admitted, what boy wouldn't gawk.

Gilbert lifted the whip hanging from his saddle. Charles's pulse hammered in his temples. He clamped his jaw, fighting the rage building at the sight of this piece of human trash uncoiling a whip. For weeks he'd heard Gilbert cracking the leather, demolishing gourds and clay pots over and over and over as he strengthened his wrist and perfected his snap. And now he wanted to crack it at a woman.

Charles's fingers closed on his own whip. With a flip of his wrist, he could wrap the length of his lash around Gilbert's neck, yank him off his mount, and drag him, Gilbert's hands clawing at his neck, his face purpling, his breath gurgling out of his throat.

No. Not yet. Cool reason cleared the vision. Control. Always control, else all would be lost before they'd taken their chance.

"I could split your belly open, girl," Gilbert said. "You know that? Might be a little green devil baby would spill out. What you think, Edmund?"

"What?" the boy said, his jaw hanging open.

Gilbert snapped the whip and opened a red slash across Celine's bare foot. "Want to see a green devil baby fall out of her belly?"

In spite of the rein Charles kept on his emotions, a wave of nausea rose up from his gut. He had seen a woman split open by a whip once. Seen the gaping womb and the unborn babe. He drew a breath, got hold of himself, and glanced at Gilbert's cousin.

4

"What?" Edmund said again, his voice high and thin. The boy's eyes were wide and unbelieving. Could be Mr. Edmund was worth saving when the time came. If it worked out that way.

"Trouble is, Mr. Gilbert ..." Charles said. He paused to give Celine a look-over like he had little interest in the scene. Her breasts were high and full of a young woman's juice, her dark belly taut and round, the navel inverted and poking out like a nipple. She had to be scared, but she kept her eyes on the ground, her face impassive. If she'd been smart, that's what she'd have done when Gilbert and the boy rode up in the first place. "Trouble is, Mr. Gilbert, you'd be depriving Mr. Andry of two valuable pieces of property. Doubt the girl would survive being opened up, and a sure thing the babe wouldn't."

Gilbert gave a nervous titter. Charles knew him for a coward, afraid of his own daddy, especially if he cost Andry a breeder and a baby. But Gilbert had a shallow man's pride, and for Celine's sake, Charles offered him a face-saving alternative.

"Why don't I take her over to the stocks, let her back cramp up for a few hours instead. You can ride by later this afternoon and take a look at her if you want. Nothing makes a face contort like a muscle spasm."

Gilbert's laugh was full of false cheer. "Very well. I'm as forgiving as the next man. Take her to the stocks. I want her dress off, though. Clamp her in tight, but leave her titties free."

The boy's face flamed red. Charles took that as a good sign. Might be he would develop a taste for slave women in a few years. Some of them did. But maybe he wouldn't use them brutally the way Gilbert did. Half the women on the place had scars on their cheeks, a notch for every time the master's son used her.

Charles nodded to Old Gus to bring her along and turned toward the quarters.

At the stocks, he dismounted and waited for Gus and Celine to catch up. His mount, a tired old quarter horse he babied like a precious pet, nudged his shoulder. He patted her absently and lit his pipe as he watched Celine amble along like she was going for a Sunday stroll. She was a tough one, Celine was. But stupid to have given Gilbert a reason to notice her.

He unlocked the stocks and gestured for her to sit down on the bench. "Take the dress off," he reminded her. It was a cold gray day, the kind that chilled to the bone, but she should have thought of that before she let herself look at Mr. Gilbert. Likely that was his baby in her belly, judging by the scar on her cheek. Guess it was hard to ignore a man who'd filled your belly with a white baby, but there was no room for pity in this world.

Wordlessly, Celine stretched her legs out so her feet stuck out over the ankle slots, leaned forward so her wrists did the same at the upper bar. Charles set his pipe down on the post, clamped the bars down on her ankles, and gave the screw a twist to keep the boards steady. When he laid the upper bar down, Celine cried out. "You got a pinch of skin in between them boards, Mr. Charles."

He released the board, let her reposition her wrists, then clamped the bar down.

"You let Maisy stay close, Mr. Charles?"

Celine had earned herself a cramped back. Carrying a slave's rage in your heart didn't excuse being stupid, but she didn't deserve Gilbert messing with her. Likely he'd behave if his old mammy stood by.

"I'll send her to you. She can put some salve on that cut."

Celine eyed the whip slash on her foot. "It ain't too bad."

Yes, she was a tough one. He stuck his pipe in his mouth and left her in the stocks, her skin pebbled with cold. She wouldn't complain, no matter how cold or how cramped, not Celine. Once Gilbert had had his look at her, Maisy standing witness, he could let her out.

The rest of the afternoon, Charles patrolled the fields where the hands were cleaning up from the last of the cane harvest. He took pride in the smooth operation of Woodlawn Plantation. He administered swift punishments when called for, and none of the slaves would call him friend. But he was fair. It was a fine line he walked. Hiding his true aims, he convinced both the master and his fellow slaves that he was the white man's creature. It wouldn't be long now, though, before they understood how false that image was.

He finished his rounds and guided his horse back to the lane running through the quarters. All the gardens were planted with winter greens and here and there a chicken scratched in the dirt. No garbage, no trash, and no reeking over-filled privies, he noted with satisfaction, then turned to the stocks to let Celine out.

A dark cloud lined the western sky. Celine would be colder than a witch's...Well, hell. That white devil Gilbert was there. Charles hadn't meant to be there when Gilbert came by to mock or pinch or whatever he had in mind. Having Charles witness it when he tormented a slave seemed to excite him all the more. A twisted creature, Gilbert Andry. But there he was, standing behind Celine, his hands squeezing her breasts.

Mr. Edmund , pale and staring atop his gray mare, looked like he tasted something foul. But that didn't keep the boy from watching his cousin molest a helpless woman. Her back was bent, her legs stretched out in front of her, her arms straight out, too. Her breasts hung down like great bells between her arms, the nipples huge. Cold had made her dark skin dusky grey and goose pimpled. She was trembling as Gilbert pinched her tender nipples, then smoothed over her great belly to probe between her legs.

Maisy stood close, her arms crossed, her eyes boring into the master's son. Behind her, three little pickaninnies sucked their fingers and watched. Charles hoped Maisy being there, along with the little ones, would keep the son of a bitch from doing anything worse.

Celine looked up at Charles, but there was no pleading in her eyes. What he saw was rage, and despair. Even if she were not bound hand and foot, what could she do to protect herself against the man who owned her hours, her labor, her very skin, bones, hair and blood? Defy the master, and end up with the skin flayed off her back? But Celine being Celine, she might still spit, or bite, or curse. He hoped she wouldn't. He wanted to steady her with a word, to keep her hate from spilling out. If he did that, though, he'd look like he was on her side, and there was too much at stake for Andry's son to see him as anything but his faithful dog.

Charles fastened his attention on Mr. Edmund. If seeing a naked woman stripped of all dignity aroused him, he'd be on the same sorry path as Gilbert. When the boy sensed his gaze, he looked over at Charles and faltered at the stone hard look Charles had perfected.

Mr. Edmund flushed and lowered his face. Maybe he deserved to live. Maybe not. No question they would kill Gilbert when the time came.

Gilbert finished his molestation by twisting Celine's nipples and laughing when she cried out. He sauntered over to his horse, but before he mounted, he rubbed his crotch and smirked at Charles.

Charles hid behind the slave's mask, his face neutral, revealing nothing of his disgust. No, there'd be no mercy for Gilbert Andry.

Gilbert tipped his hat at Maisy. "You have a nice afternoon, Mammy."

He rode off with Mr. Edmund following behind. The boy turned for one more look at Celine, his face openly sorrowful. Charles had a weak moment, hoping this cousin would be back in Baton Rouge when it was time. But if he were not, well, he would get what they all got.

Maisy stepped forward and wrapped a quilt around Celine's shoulders. Charles dismounted to free her from the stocks and caught Celine staring after Gilbert, hatred beaming from her eyes.

"Get that look off your face," he snapped at her, harsh as the whip. She'd earn herself a striping yet if she didn't learn to control herself.

She lowered her eyes and made her face into her own slave's mask.

Charles unlocked the bars and stepped aside to see if she could stand. She tried, and fell to her knees, moaning as cramps seized her legs and back. He hefted her into his arms, the blanket falling away.

"You just want a look at my titties, Mr. Charles."

Charles laughed out loud, a rare moment for him. She was a warrior woman, this one. And that was her way of saying thank you.

He carried her to her cabin, Maisy stepping along beside him. "You got anything warming on the fire?" he asked the old woman.

"Yessir. I gots a pot of hot greens cooking. They'll warm her up. And while she eat that, I'll boil her some grits. She be all right."

Evening turned the shadows blue, then black. Charles stood on the porch of his cabin, set fifty yards from the rest of the quarters. The air smelled of wood smoke and frying fat back, of collard greens and mutton. He heard children laughing, some man's sweet baritone singing. Every slave on the place sat with other slaves, talking, sharing the day.

Loneliness closed in on him. For a moment he thought of walking through the night air to one of the cabins, Yvette's maybe. He could have any woman in the quarters, who would say him nay? But that was just it. No one would turn him away. And he'd feel like Gilbert Andry. Besides, it wasn't Yvette he wanted.

Charles lived a life dislocated from every other soul on the Andry plantation. The master treated him well, spoke to him like he was next thing to a human being. But Charles was no toady, pleased to be in the great man's presence. While he said his *yessirs* and dipped his head in deference, he imagined the man's head lying at his feet. Imagined the man's lands enriched by his own blood, lands the slaves would soon own. Yet neither was Charles invited to sit with the other slaves on a Sunday evening to tell stories and sing songs. He was a slave as they were, but it was his job to spur the lazy and punish the defiant. He was an extension of Manuel Andry, a hand of the master. Yet his competence earned him a cabin of his own set off from the quarters, the license to come and go, and the opportunity to conspire.

The night air nipping at him, Charles walked out into the yard and turned his back on the quarters, his face toward the big house. Through the pecan grove, he could see the yellow glow of a hundred candles lit for Mr. Andry's guests. Over the strains of the fiddles, tinkling laughter floated. The fine ladies, their skin fragrant with talcum powder, their white hands smooth and soft, would be in their pretty silks.

A sudden rectangle of light winked as the outer door of the master's office opened. *Here he comes. With a friend, this time.* He stepped back onto his porch in the deeper shadows as Andry held the lantern high, gliding through the night on his way to the quarters. Which cabin, that was the question.

Damnation. Charles leapt off the porch. It'd be Baby Ann's cabin. She and Caleb had jumped the broom last Sunday, and Andry wouldn't resist the chance to remind every slave on the place that, wedding or not, each one of them belonged to him.

Charles strode toward the cabin. Caleb was no George. He would not step out and meekly leave his woman for the master's pleasure.

Charles cut through Maisy's back garden, hopped over a low fence, and knocked on Baby Ann's back door while Andry's lantern still bobbed through the pecan grove.

"Caleb," he whispered.

Caleb opened the door, hardly visible in the night. "That you, Mr. Charles?"

"Come out here. Close the door."

"What you need this time of night, Mr. Charles?"

"I need you to come out here."

9

Caleb stepped into the yard. Then he spied the lantern and the two shadowy, well-fed figures coming down the lane. He went still, watching. He turned his head to Charles, then back toward the master's familiar form, figuring it out.

Rage, sudden and explosive, erupted as Caleb sprinted for the two men. Charles lunged for him, caught him around the knees. They both went down. Caleb kicked, then threw his hard fists at Charles.

"Stop it, you damn fool," Charles hissed. "You'll get yourself whipped, or worse."

Charles clambered up Caleb's body until he had him pinned by the shoulders. With his hard hand clamped on Caleb's mouth, he whispered in his ear. "You think Baby Ann wants you killed? You think she can't handle a couple of old white farts? Be smart, Caleb. Be smart, and you won't be dead."

They could hear the master's step on the front porch. Caleb tried to heave Charles off, but Charles was ready for him.

"I have to knock you out to keep you alive? You'll get him. When the time comes, Andry is yours. I promise."

Caleb's body went slack.

"You got hold of yourself?"

Caleb nodded. Charles rolled off him. "Go on over to the bachelors' cabin for the night. Tomorrow, you can work off all the steam you got built up."

Caleb climbed to his feet. "You promise?"

"Yeah. He's yours."

Chapter Two

Charles slipped through the woods to the edge of the swamp, a bright three quarters moon and plenty of stars lighting the way. Far back into the wilds beyond the Trouard plantation, a glimmer pulled him to the clearing where Kook, Quamana and Mathurin warmed themselves.

He stood at the edge of the circle of light, anger flickering inside him. "You've lit a fire."

Quamana rose and turned to face the accusation, his body taut, ready.

Mathurin stepped in front of Quamana, his hands loose at his sides. "It's cold, Charles. Nobody will see this little fire. Come sit with us, warm your hands."

Charles's gaze swept over his confederates. Kook on the ground, loose-limbed and relaxed. Quamana, towering over all of them, glaring. And Mathurin, the peacekeeper, offering a hint of a smile to placate him. Able men, proven men, he reminded himself. He should not be so quick to criticize.

He folded his long legs and joined them. The heat felt good on his palms as he held them out. He waited. Mathurin would be the first to speak. He couldn't hold it in, Mathurin couldn't.

"Did you bring the book?"

"I said I would."

"I thought we should read some of it. Aloud. For Kook and Quamana. They'll tell it to the others when they can."

"That's what worries me. Too much talk, the wrong ears hear it."

From the corner of his eye, he saw Quamana stiffen.

"He don't mean you, Quamana," Kook said easily, a grin playing over his features. "He means me."

"I trust Kook with my life," Quamana said.

"So do we all," Mathurin put in. "We have to trust each other, or we have nothing. Charles. Why do you insult us?"

Mathurin was a man much like himself. His mother had been a black slave, his father a white planter. That much was not unusual. But Mathurin too could read. He could think and plan. Charles turned his gaze on Quamana. The raised scars on his cheeks and forehead marked him as an Akan warrior of the Asante people. Charles had seen him laboring in the fields, his face a mask that disguised his shrewd intelligence and the fury in his heart. Here, away from white eyes, he did not conceal the tension in his shoulders and hands, the heat in his eyes. Rage seethed under the black skin.

Charles stared hard at Kook. The young man's hands hung loosely over his knees, his posture as care-free as if they had come together to share a jar of rough whiskey. Scarification proved he had been a blooded Akan warrior as well, yet his features were soft and pretty as a woman's. Along with Quamana, he had survived the passage across the ocean jammed in with sick and dying people, rats, and filth, yet he smiled readily.

In Kook's eyes Charles had never seen a hint of the anger that simmered in Quamana, in Mathurin, in himself. In all the conspirators. And there was that easy smile again.

"You think I am a boy, Charles Deslondes. You make this clear," Kook said in his genial manner. "I can prove to you it is not so, if you like."

"How would you do that?"

"Many ways. I could fight you and lay you down in the dirt, my knife at your throat. I could tear a man's throat out with my teeth—you can choose the man."

Charles didn't take the challenge. No question Kook was strong. Taller than Charles, younger.

"No? Then I show you my other strength, the kind that is in the mind."

Kook stretched his arm over the fire. He lowered his palm until it hovered just above the flames. Charles watched him. Nothing showed in his face. Not pain, not effort. Kook lowered his palm so that flame licked the skin. Charles smelled his flesh burn, and still Kook betrayed nothing in his face.

Mathurin slapped Kook's arm away from the fire. Angrily, Mathurin held up the palm's burned flesh to Charles. "You of all people should know that what a slave shows the world is not what is in his heart."

He looked at Kook, whose expression was as mild and easy as it had been before he held his hand over the fire. Charles smiled. "That must hurt like hell."

Kook smiled back at him. "It does."

"He is a man," Quamana murmured.

Kook answered, as quietly as Quamana, "I am a man."

Charles had heard these two Africans in their ritual of quiet defiance before this. It was a mantra between the two of them and always brought echoes of Charles's deepest memory.

He reached into his breast pocket and withdrew a battered blue book. He placed it in Kook's hand. "You hold one of the great books of the world."

Kook ran his fingers over the faded letters on the cover. "What are these words?"

"*Declaration of the Rights of Man and of the Citizen.* Written by the French people throwing off the oppression of their king."

Kook passed the book to Quamana who opened it at random. His fingers traced a line of print, then turned to another page and did the same. "Tell us some of these words."

Charles nodded toward Mathurin, who accepted the book from Quamana. For a moment, he simply held it in his hands. "Before I read, I will tell you what is most important. Men have inborn natural rights, to property, to liberty, and to life."

"White men have said this," Quamana said.

"Yes. In France. And in the United States. Learned men. Passionate men."

Quamana gestured toward the book. "Tell us."

Mathurin turned to the first page and began to read. The night was quiet, the gators buried in mud, the insects asleep.

"People of accomplishment," Mathurin read, "want their personal liberty and protection of it, while some others, or an association of others, want to displace them. Yet all individuals have the right to remain at the locus assigned them by nature…"

Charles had read the words many times and allowed his gaze at the fire to blur, his attention to turn inward. At his mother's knee, he too had been taught a mantra.

Maybe six years old, Charles had squatted, his stick drawing aimless spirals in the dust. Flies buzzed around his head, but he ignored them. He ignored the sounds coming from the cabin behind him, too. Always the bed ropes groaned, the man panted, and then he'd grunt one long sigh and it was over. Maman made no noise at all. She had promised him it didn't hurt.

The white man came out of Maman's cabin buttoning his pants. "Hey, there, boy." He dug in his pocket and held his closed hand out, palm down. "What you think I got here for you?"

Charles's gaze flicked over the hand and lit on the man's red face, on his tiny blue eyes. Master, Maman called him.

"Cat got your tongue, eh? Stand up here and see what I brought you."

Charles didn't want what was in the man's hand, whatever it was. Once it had been a beautiful shell lined with nacre. Another time it was a biscuit gone crumbly and stale.

His mother stood in her doorway. "Charles," she said. "Stand up. Wipe your hands off."

Charles stood. His head came no higher than the man's elbow, but he didn't feel small. His bare dusky chest was skinny, his legs and arms thin, but he had room inside for a great, secret rage.

He wiped his hands on the threadbare pants that came to just below his knees.

"That's better," the man said. "Now hold your hand out."

Charles knew what he was supposed to do. He held his hand out.

"Here you are, young man. Charles, isn't it?"

The master dropped a brilliant red gem in his hand. Charles felt himself drawn into the candy, the sun lighting it up from inside, the red suffusing across his palm. It was beautiful, maybe the most beautiful thing he'd ever seen.

"Watch his face when he tastes that, then," the man said.

Charles didn't want to eat it. He wanted to keep it safe, among his feathers and shells under the mattress, so he could take it out and look at in the sunshine.

"Go on, boy. Eat it."

The immediate flood of sweetness zinged through his mouth, deep into his tongue, down his throat and up behind his nose. He closed his eyes. He felt weakened. He felt like crying. He didn't want this, not from the master. Something like this, a sensation to melt away all the hate a boy stored up, shouldn't come from *him*.

"Best thing you ever tasted, eh, boy?"

"Charles," Maman said. "Thank Master for the candy."

He felt his throat had closed up. He tried to wet his lips, the candy dissolving on his tongue. Sweet. Incredibly sweet.

"Thank you, Master," he managed.

"Good boy. You teach him his manners, Marie, he won't have to go out in the cane."

"Yes, sir, Master. Just like you promised."

"You're a good girl, Marie." He took a moment to admire the blue sky and puffy white clouds, and as far as the eye could see, acres of green cane swaying in the breeze. "Yes, sir, a paradise, that's what we have here." The master adjusted his hat, then headed for the big house where his wife and children waited dinner on him.

"Come in here," Maman said, all the softness gone from her voice.

Charles followed her in. Maman sat on the bed and Charles stood before her. Her pretty smile was gone now, her ebony skin darker than the shadows.

"You know what you got to do."

Tears pooled in Charles eyes, but he would never shed them. He leaned over, stuck his finger down his throat, and vomited up a stream of red ropy syrup onto the dirt floor. The sweetness had been ruined in his stomach. It came up vile and sour, the sweet notes sickening now. He wiped his mouth with the back of his hand.

Maman kicked dust on the sticky mess with her bare foot. Then she took him by the arms and brought him close. "Whose skin you got, Charles?"

"Yours. And his."

"Who are you under that skin, Charles?"

"I'm a man, Maman."

"That's right. You are a man, Charles. You do what you got to do. You eat his candy. You take his trinkets. You never let him see *you*. You too smart for that. You too deep for that."

She tightened her grip on his arms, but he didn't flinch. "Who are you, Charles?"

"I'm a black man, Maman."

Mathurin's voice cut into his remembrance of that day so long ago, yet even now, Charles thought as he gazed into the fire, he would expunge the whiteness from his blood if he could. He wanted no part of the white man's privileges and assumptions. He wanted no part of their corruption. Even when he snapped the whip at a black man's back, he felt pure at heart. He did it for the greater goal. He did it for all of them, for all of the black men and women and their children. And the goal would be reached soon. He could feel the moments moving ever more swiftly, feel the tension growing. Soon.

Mathurin closed the book.

Kook said, "It is death to be caught with this book."

"Yes."

"It is death to be caught saying these words."

"Yes."

A smile lit Kook's too-pretty face. "I will whisper, then, when I tell the others."

"We'll meet again, behind Andry's place, Sunday night." Charles looked at each man in turn. "No fire."

"You worry too much," Kook dared to tease.

"And I'm still alive."

Chapter Three

Charles kicked dirt into the fire until he was sure it was extinguished, then followed his confederates back through the woods. Up and down the river road, scores of plantations stretched between Andry's Woodlawn plantation and New Orleans. To allow each planter access to the river, the properties were narrow, some no more than 500 feet wide, though each stretched far back into the country where the forest had been cleared for cane and cotton. Using the rutted lanes that crossed these back acres, it took only minutes to traverse one plantation and move into the next.

Mathurin returned to his own cabin in the quarters of the Trouard plantation. The others moved through the lane like ghosts, not even the dogs noticing them. Charles's master Andry's place lay upriver, but Charles stayed with Kook and Quamana as they picked up the lane heading to the Brown plantation. There Kook and Quamana disappeared into their cabins.

Charles continued on to Trépagnier's place. He slipped through the night and at last stepped softly onto Annique's little porch. He pulled off his boots and eased inside. The fire had burned down to embers, but he let it be. She likely only had enough wood on hand for the morning's breakfast. They'd be warm enough snuggled in bed together.

He shucked off his canvas pants, his jacket and his shirt and crawled in beside her. She draped her arm over his chest and pulled herself close. "Your feet are cold," she murmured. He smoothed her hair and kissed her forehead. "Go back to sleep."

Before dawn, she woke him, her work-roughened hands sliding over his ribs. He turned to her. "Annique," he whispered. Only with Annique, only with this woman, had he ever allowed feeling in. He threaded his fingers through her hair, gripping her as he deepened his kiss. His woman. His Annique.

Afterwards, they lay together, sated and content as the winter sun lightened the window. Annique tightened her arm around his chest. "Don't go yet," she mumbled against his back.

He twisted in her arms. "No, not yet." Now he could see her in the pearly light. Her dark eyes, slightly tilted, her high rounded cheeks, and her mouth, soft and pink, smiling at him. "What you smiling at this morning?"

"You. Sleeping in my arms, big tough Charles Deslondes, sweet as a baby."

He kissed her nose. "You keep it to yourself and I'll give you a reward."

"Yeah? What you give me?"

He ducked under the cover, nibbling his way over her breasts and belly as her throaty laugh rumbled in his ear.

It was full light when Charles left the bed. His own early morning chores back at Andry's were in George's capable hands. He would ring the bell and assign the crews their tasks as Charles had laid them out the day before. Annique would soon have to start the big vats boiling at the laundry shed, but first he'd build her a fire.

As the cabin warmed, he dressed, then sat on the edge of the bed to pull on his boots. "You a sleepy-head this morning?" he said.

Annique rolled over. "Seems like all I want to do is sleep these dark mornings. But don't go. I'm gone fix your breakfast."

Charles glanced out the window at the weak sun. "All right." He slapped her quilt-covered rump. "Best get at it, lazy bones." In response to the scratch on the door, he got up to open it for Annique's old gray tabby to sashay in.

He stood in the middle of the room buckling his belt, the cat winding between his legs. Annique climbed out from under the covers and walked across the floor to him. He dropped his hands to watch her in all her naked splendor. Long arms and slender legs, high breasts, and a smile on her face. She wrapped her arms around his neck.

"Charles Deslondes. Will you jump the broom with me?"

His hands on her waist, he felt his heart freeze.

Annique's pretty smile vanished. She dropped her arms from his neck. "You look like you just swallowed a lemon."

What could he say? He could be dead in a few weeks. Probably would be. But he didn't want her to know about that. He didn't want her involved at all. If they failed, and in his darker moments he figured the odds were that they would fail, there would be whippings, and killings. What she didn't know couldn't hurt her.

She stepped back. "I thought..." She wouldn't look at him.

He'd hurt her. He pulled her close, made her let him hold her, and breathed in her warm scent. His head told him no, it was foolish for him to marry, anyone, ever. But for once he could hear his heart speak. Before he died, would it be so wrong to belong to someone? To have someone who belonged to him? With Annique in his arms, an unfamiliar twinge shot through him. He might live. They might have a future together.

His hand in her hair, his lips at her ear, he told her the truth. "You are my light, Annique. My hope." He tilted her face up and kissed her gently. "I will be proud to jump the broom with you."

Her dark eyes were still worried. "You sure?"

"I'm sure. I'm just a fool not to have said it first. Don't doubt me, Annique. You are my heart."

She pressed her hand to his chest. "And you are mine."

He kissed her, her beautiful body pressed to him, and began to walk her back toward the bed.

She laughed. "I'll be late getting the tubs boiling."

"We'll skip breakfast."

When they finally left the cabin, Annique touched his hand. "You'll speak to the master?"

He nodded. "I got business up there with Trépagnier this morning. I'll talk to him."

The smile she gave him lit her eyes, her face, and his entire being. He gave her a quick kiss and a grin and let her run off to the laundry.

Charles walked from the quarters through the orchard to the back door of the big house belonging to Annique's master, one of the most hated men on the River Road. It curdled Charles' stomach every time he had to talk to the man, but Andry had sent him with business to discuss.

Dominique, Trépagnier's head house slave, let him in. "Master's having breakfast, but he expecting you. You go on in."

Charles put his hat on the back hall table and walked into the breakfast room, Dominique trailing behind him with the coffee pot. The morning sun lit the pale yellow walls and the crystal bowl of camellias on the table. The linen tablecloth, most likely boiled and bleached and ironed by Annique's own hands, glowed softly white. And presiding over this lovely room, François Trépagnier sat drinking coffee. The *Louisiana Gazette* lay folded next to his plate of beignets. The slave Gustave knelt on the floor at his master's feet, attentive and eager, like a dog waiting for a scrap.

Trépagnier smiled as Dominique refilled his coffee cup. "Good morning, Charles. You've brought the proposal for the sawmill?"

"Yes, sir." He handed Trépagnier the envelope from his breast pocket. This was a project Charles had been maneuvering his master toward for some time, as subtly as he could manage. He was fairly certain that by now Andry thought the mill was his own idea, including sharing the costs with his crony. "Mr. Andry figures you can both make a profit. He asks you to look over these figures at your leisure."

Trépagnier opened the envelope and examined the page. With his free hand, his attention on the proposal, he broke off a piece of beignet and tossed it toward Gustave.

Gustave lunged to catch it with his mouth, but he missed. Before he could snatch it up with claw-like fingers, Trépagnier said, "No."

Gustave settled back on his heels, but his eyes lingered on the scrap of pastry on the floor. The boy--though in truth, if he had been a normal human being, he would be a young man – the boy had the vacant gaze of a simpleton. Whether he had been born or made that way, Charles did not know. But what would it do to a human soul to be trained and treated like a dog?

Trépagnier continued to read as Charles stood waiting and Gustave maintained his pose. At a slight noise from Dominique, Charles looked at him. The head house slave, dressed in woolen livery, clean and pressed, smirked and nodded at Gustave. The boy wore a threadbare shirt and short pants on this cold morning, no shoes, but around his neck was a well-oiled leather collar with bright shiny half-inch spikes. A dog's collar.

When Charles did not respond to Dominique's smirk, the man tried again. He nodded at Gustave and sneered, expecting Charles to enjoy the cruelty along with him and the master. Charles forced his hands to remain open, but his mind leapt to murder. Dominique would not survive the revolt when it came.

Charles glanced at Gustave, and for an instant, he thought he saw a glimmer of intelligence, a hint of rage in the boy's eye as he caught Dominique's contempt. And then it was gone. Maybe he'd imagined it.

"I'll pen a reply and send it over with Dominique this afternoon," Trépagnier said.

"Yes, sir. There is another matter as well."

Trépagnier reached for the marmalade pot.

"Sir, your girl Annique is my woman. We want to jump the broom together."

"Do you now?"

"Yes, sir."

"She good in the sack, spread her legs real wide, does she?" he said as he spooned marmalade on his beignet.

Charles stared at Trépagnier's chin as if the master had not spoken.

"She got a good ass on her, that one does." He bit into the beignet, marmalade smearing his lips. "Bet she's got pretty tits."

Charles felt the acid rise in his gullet. He focused on his inner eye, a vision of Trépagnier with a machete at his throat.

The man chuckled. "About time she dropped some young 'uns. Course she'll stay here, do her work like always, and her little niggers will belong to me." He slapped his hand on the table in decision. "Tell Andry it's all right with me if it's all right with him."

"Thank you, sir."

Trépagnier looked him over from head to foot. "You a good specimen, yourself. I expect you'll make me some fine little nigger babies. Yes. You have my blessing."

"Thank you, sir," Charles said again. "I'll tell Mr. Andry you're sending a reply later today." He dipped his head and left the room.

In the hallway, he walked steadily to the table, picked up his hat and put it on. Dominique was behind him, but even if he'd been alone in the hall, Charles would not have shown even a suggestion of the violence in his heart.

"Don't that beat all, that Gustave? He ain't no more than a dog, yapping his mouth open to catch a scrap." Dominique chuckled. "Lucky he don't get kicked every time he miss. Keeps me and the master entertained, he does."

Charles stared at him, unblinking. Did he think he and the master were friends? Had he forgotten he was a slave, just as

Gustave was? The man's balls must have shrunk to the size of peas.

Instead of shaking his head, Charles shrugged. "Boy's not nearly as much fun as a good hound dog, seems to me."

Dominique's nose went up. His tone turned frosty. "Good morning to you," he said, and opened the door. Charles passed through without a glance at the soulless piece of shit.

Chapter Four

Kook and Quamana and a dozen other men and women hoed the lush dark earth in preparation for the nubs of sugar cane they'd plant in January. The day was bright and clear and cool, the air scented with the rich dirt with a hint of salt air from the faraway Gulf. Sea gulls wheeled overhead having followed the great river to this land of streams and bayous.

Crawley, the yellow-headed overseer, rode his horse down the lane, his flat eyes lazily scanning the slaves. Kook didn't tense up. He never tensed up. But he watched, alert for trouble. He himself rarely had any trouble with anyone. He made it a point to be friendly, malleable, stupid. *Whatever you say, Massa*. That was his defense. That was his pose. But Kook had to keep an eye on Quamana.

Only five years before, Kook had been a young recruit under the great Quamana's command. Then came capture, and enslavement. A week after the sailing ship had left the African coast with its human cargo, the captain had the slaves brought on deck in small teams to be exercised. No profit in delivering shrunken, wizened creatures to the auction block. At the top of the stairs leading to the deck, Kook had paused, holding up the exodus of men from the bowels of the ship. He raised his face to the sun, closing his eyes. The light and the fresh sea air made him giddy after days in the fetid dark hold, crammed in with other miserable souls, too crowded to turn over, too chained to stand, sit, or stretch. Reveling in the warmth on his eyelids, he breathed in deeply.

"Get your arse out here, nigger," a red-faced sailor snarled at him as he slammed the flat side of his blade against Kook's buttocks.

Kook whirled round to take the cutlass from the sailor. He could have done it, in spite of his chains. He was fifteen years old. A man. A warrior. Young, but he had earned his pride charging into his king's enemies with his spear raised. He could cut this man in half with his own blade. But there were other sailors with blades and guns. Kook stepped out of the way.

A man beat a drum and another played a flute while Kook and the other slaves were made to jump, to run in a circle, to wave their arms in the air, all under the careful gazes of sailors armed with muskets and swords. With him in this group was Quamana, older by five years, tall and strong and fearless. Quamana had been a captain in the great Asante army, and Kook had eagerly followed him into the final battle that had cost them their freedom.

In the days they'd been aboard, Kook had been unable to keep the foul food down, but he had tried to swallow it. Quamana would not even try. He seemed to smolder in his chains, his arms and legs tense as if at any moment he would leap up and break the iron bonds with his bare hands.

On deck, Quamana jumped and ran with stiff, jerky limbs. Kook knew his captain. He had lain next to him in chains these days and nights and felt the rage simmering under the skin, and so he watched him, his leader, his hero. Whatever Quamana did, Kook would do. That's how it had been in the war. And now, if Quamana chose to attack these filthy sailors and die doing it, then Kook would, too.

But there was the sun on his skin, the fresh breeze blowing away the stink on his body. The blue sky overhead was infinite, endless and timeless. Kook didn't want to die.

Across the deck, Kook caught sight of Quamana's face as they ran in a tight circle. His eyes were focused on the man standing on the half-deck above with a sword in his hand. A barrel sat just below the man. An easy leap onto the barrel, over the low railing to the man. Easy to take the sword, to slash that sailor, then the next, and another and another until Quamana was himself shot and slashed. An honorable death. A warrior's death.

Kook couldn't let him do it. Quamana was crazed with anger, he wasn't thinking. There would be better opportunities to rebel, better chances to win their freedom without dying. When they were off this ship. When they had a plan.

Kook faked a muscle cramp in his calf. He staggered out of the line, pushing himself across the circle and lunging into Quamana. Quamana tried to shove him off and make his move for the sailor on the upper deck, but Kook seized him around the hips and made his body a dead weight.

The sailors rushed them, shouting at them, pounding them with the butts of their guns and the hilts of their swords. Kook let go of Quamana and rolled off him to shield his head from the onslaught, to make it clear he submitted. But not Quamana. He roared from the depths of his belly. He swung those hardened fists into a jaw, a nose, a gut all the while the blows fell on his shoulders and arms and ribs. Those three sailors were joined by two more and still Quamana fought, bloodying and tearing at his assailants. Then a man raised a belaying pin and slammed it into the back of Quamana's head. He went down as if he were dead.

The sailors stood back. The captain wouldn't like it if they'd killed a prime slave like this one, but if they had, they'd slip him over the side for the sharks like they did all the weak ones who couldn't survive down below. The man with the belaying pin looked toward the captain's cabin door, then bent over to feel for a pulse at Quamana's neck.

"He's alive. Get him down below. Double chains. And don't let him on deck no more."

Kook lay next to Quamana when he and the others were taken back down into the hold. The bleeding from Quamana's many wounds had stopped, even the massive clotted mass on the back of his head. But he lay unconscious all that day and through the night. When the water bucket came round, Kook dribbled water into Quamana's mouth and massaged his throat to make him swallow.

When Quamana woke, he looked at Kook with dazed eyes. He tried to raise his hand to his head and discovered he was chained. He frowned, perplexed. Kook held his breath, afraid Quamana would fight the iron, roar out his anger, and bring the sailors down on them. But before Quamana could fully understand his predicament, his eyes closed and he lapsed again into unconsciousness.

Quamana remained like this for days. Kook lost track of how many. He spooned a little gruel in his mouth and as much water as he could get. Quamana didn't die, and he didn't live, but when he at last awoke, there was no confusion in his eyes. He understood exactly where he was and what had happened to him.

"You fell on me on purpose," he said to Kook.

"Yes."

Quamana turned his head away and closed his eyes.

If he could move away, Kook thought, it would be better. Let Quamana have his anger and hate, even if it were directed at him. But that he couldn't do. He could not even turn his back to his beloved captain. So he closed his eyes, too. Anyway, it was easier to live another minute and then another if he didn't look at the deadened gazes of the men and women around him. If he could manage not to breathe the horrid stench, he would do that, too. Somewhere over on the women's platform, a sweet voice began a low mournful song, and Kook dived deep into that river of sweetness and let his mind swim into the dark cool depths.

Over the next days, Kook slowly realized Quamana was not the same man he had been. As a captain, he'd been brave, but he'd been thoughtful before committing himself or his men to an action. He'd kept a cool head even while covered in blood, his enemies' and his own. Now the rage flowed just under the skin so that the slightest insult sent Quamana into a fury.

The poor soul on the other side of Quamana had in his sleep jerked the chain that bound them together so that the iron cuff around Quamana's ankle dug into the perpetual sores they all suffered. Quamana hauled against the chain on his wrist, yanking all the arms down the row attached to the same chain, and lunged for the man's throat. The struggle was short, but terrifying. Kook, fearing he'd rip the man's throat out, pounded on his shoulder, even bit into the muscle below Quamana's neck.

The short squat sailor on guard duty rushed over at the shouting and lashed his whip on Quamana's legs, catching Kook's and the victim's legs as well. At the terrible cuts from the whip Quamana released his fellow captive and tried to lunge at the sailor. The chains kept him on his back as the whip cut into the bottoms of Quamana's feet. He roared, crazed with pain and fury.

Kook raised his head, all he could manage in the tight bindings, and recognized the Portuguese who sometimes opened the portals to give them a breath of air. "Mumbo! Stop! Let me quiet him. Just stop!" The other slaves' voices joined his till there was a cacophony of outrage at the man with the whip. Unperturbed, Mumbo coiled his leather and waddled back to his post at the top of the stairs.

Ignoring the pain where the whip had caught him, Kook shuffled his body so he could talk quietly to Quamana. "You have to listen to me, Quamana. It's me. Kook. Your friend. Your brother in this hellhole. Remember who you are. You are an Asante. You will have your power back. But you have to control the rage." On and on Kook whispered, saying the same things in many ways, calling Quamana back to himself. And finally, he felt the tension in Quamana's body lessen. "You are a man," Kook whispered.

"I am a man," Quamana answered. He closed his eyes and put himself into a kind of trance. When Mumbo commanded they shift to reduce the incidence of terrible pressure sores from lying on the hard boards, he would roll to his side with the whole line of bodies. He ate a few bites of the swill they were offered, drank the nasty water passed out to them; otherwise, he was a man in limbo. Kook whispered to him for the weeks of hell in the stinking hold. "We will survive. We will be free. We are Asante. We are men."

The last day of the voyage, the African men and women caught the smell of land wafting down the passageway. The ordeal was nearly over. The hold was considerably less crowded now after so many of them had succumbed to despair. Kook had seen his nearest neighbor choose death as clearly as if he had leapt over the side of the boat. He refused food and water, he refused to talk or to listen. Within three days, Mumbo had hauled his body off the planks and up on deck. Kook had heard his body splash into the water and tried not to think about the sharks that followed the ship.

With the scent of land in the air, Quamana took one huge breath and revived himself from the awful gray nothingness he'd been in. He turned his head and gazed at Kook. "*You* are a man," he said.

Kook's chest had swelled with pride.

They had survived the voyage, and then the shock of being taken off the ship into good air. They were given fresh food and freedom of movement within a large sunny enclosure. They were given medical salves for their wounds and clean water to bathe in. Kook knew they meant only to heal them and fatten them up before the auction, but he made sure he and Quamana used the salves, ate the fruit and the meat. The day of the auction, the whites made them rub their skin with oil to make it shine, made them cover unhealed sores with iron rust and gunpowder to earn top dollar for their cargo.

Kook and Quamana did earn top dollar, for their strong bodies had recovered. Kook soon realized, however, the wounds to Quamana's soul would never heal. And now they hoed this rich Louisiana soil, physically strong, mentally strong, waiting for their chance. He couldn't let Quamana get himself thrown into the plantation's jail or beaten senseless just because he couldn't hold his temper. They needed him when the day came, and the day was coming.

So Kook watched the overseer turn his horse down the row next to Quamana's, Quamana working with his back to Crawley. The horse was big, its sides wider than the trough between the hoed mounds. If the overseer kept his course, and Quamana kept to his row, the horse would knock into Quamana. Closer now, Crawley moved his mount closer.

Kook dropped his hoe. He sprinted over the soft earth, triangulating the horse, Quamana, and himself. He had to get to Quamana before the horse nudged him aside. Before Quamana felt the blind red rage take him, before he could haul the overseer to the ground and slash him with the blade hidden beneath his shirt.

Kook leapt the last few feet. As he was in midair, the side of the horse, along with the overseer's boot in the stirrup, shoved Quamana aside. Kook's arms closed around Quamana and took him down.

Quamana twisted under him, furious, his fists pummeling him. Kook took the blows, wrestling him to keep him from going after the overseer. The horse ambled on down the row, oblivious, but Crawley turned in the saddle and delivered a smirk.

Kook whispered in Quamana's ear, urgent and low: "Say it with me. Until the lion—say it! Until the lion is ready to attack..."

Quamana finished the Asante adage with him. "...he does not show his teeth."

"It's not time, Quamana. Hold it in."

The breath steamed out of Quamana's nostrils, but the heaving of his chest slowed. Kook looked at his eyes. He was in control again.

How many times did this happen up and down the river, Kook wondered. A brave, strong man, pushed beyond what his pride could bear, struck back and then paid for it with bone-deep lashes, or branding, or maiming. It was worse in the summer, he'd noticed, when the heat beat down on a man's head and the salty sweat stung a thousand mosquito bites. Any man's temper rose to the surface then, as if the sun sucked it out of his marrow.

If he'd been half-delirious with heat and thirst and stinging insects, maybe Kook would have helped Quamana drag the overseer off his horse. Today was cool, though, yet Quamana's rage had overwhelmed him. How much longer could they wait? The tension, the waiting, the constant readiness kept a man's nerves taut.

Chapter Five

On Saturday, Charles rode a wagon out of the yard at first light. He was headed to New Orleans forty miles downriver to do Andry's business, and his own. This time of year it was no hardship to drive a wagon all day. The sky was blue with a few gauzy white clouds, and the breeze was mild. Once the sun rose, he was warm enough. To his right, the levee cut off his view of the river, but he could smell the water and hear it lapping against the banks.

To his left, every few hundred feet was another plantation house. Some were grand as palaces with formal gardens, the camellias blooming, the front dooryards as peaceful as a Sunday morning. Deeper into the property behind the big houses, though, men and women bent over hoes, swung axes, boiled laundry. Now and then he could hear the clang of a smithy's hammer.

Plenty of traffic on the river road on a Saturday. No other way to get to town except on the river itself. Barges and rafts big as houses carried goods downstream; fighting the current to get upstream was a struggle though, so most folks used the roads either side of the Mississippi for routine travel. Charles nodded at the travelers headed the opposite direction, unless they were white, and spoke to a few men he knew carrying kegs of nails or chests of fine goods in their wagons.

Mid-afternoon he reached the Henderson place fifteen miles above New Orleans and drove past the big house to the stables. A boy took the mule on into the barn and Charles stretched his back.

He found Harry Kenner in the carpentry shop carving an angel into a plank of pine. Charles watched him a moment. "You're pretty good with that chisel."

"This is true," Kenner said without taking his attention from the cherubic cheek he was shaping.

"What's it for?"

"Chair back."

In the years Charles had known Kenner, he'd yet to hear him string more than half a dozen words together, yet intelligence and purpose lay below the unsociable surface. With both daring and caution, Kenner had assembled a group of a dozen English speaking slaves who would rise with them when Charles gave the word, reason enough to earn Charles's respect.

"I'll leave you to it then."

Charles called in at the overseer's cabin to make his presence known. He left word with his missus and then headed for the kitchen where he charmed the cook out of an early dinner. Afterwards, he wandered over to the levee and climbed to the top of the grassy berm. A clear day like this, he could see all the way to New Orleans, even see the spires of the St. Louis Cathedral. When he'd been a growing lad, he'd had the chance a few times to be in town on a Sunday when slaves congregated at Congo Square to dance and sing and trade. What he'd seen, and done, after sunset in the shadows--he smiled at the memories of willing women, plentiful rum, heady drums and flutes. Maybe someday he would take Annique. Maybe.

He headed back to the barn. He'd be welcome to bunk with the slaves in the bachelor cabin, or with Kenner, but it was best if he kept some distance. He laid his bedroll in a pile of hay in the loft, covered his eyes with his hat, and went to sleep.

At the hoot of an owl, Charles wakened fully. That was Kenner's signal.

Outside, Charles tipped his head to gaze at a sky so full of stars they ran together in a milky haze.

"This way," Kenner said quietly. Together they walked through the night.

Charles breathed in the smell of wood smoke. Though cold nipped at his fingertips, he was at ease, slipping through the dark. This was his true life, unseen, unknown.

Behind the quarters, far back in the plantation, they met Lavaro on the edge of the woods. The three of them entered the gloom of the trees and stopped in a glade where they sat on stumps.

"How many can you count on?" Charles asked the third man.

"I count thirty-one for sure this end of the river. Six from the Krupke place, two from the Kohlers. Five from the Barrineaus, three at the Arpins, and a dozen here counting Kenner and me."

Charles nodded.

"What's the count upriver?" Kenner asked.

"Sixty, maybe seventy, to start with," Charles said. "We'll gather up more as we march."

"When?"

Charles looked at Kenner. He let the seconds pass.

"When?" Kenner insisted.

"I'll let you know."

"We're ready, you know that."

Charles nodded. They were all sick of being ready. They lived every day unbearably ready, like a race horse pawing the ground, waiting for the gun to go off.

"After the new year." Kenner deserved that much. He was a linchpin in the organization Charles had set in place.

Kenner scoffed. "That could be any time from January to July."

"I'll let you know," Charles repeated.

Kenner yielded and the talk moved on to weapons and drum signals. About the need for secrecy. Plenty of slaves would barter the lives of their fellows for the reward of a pair of shoes or an extra blanket. Some had even gone over: They believed the master and his family depended on them. They believed the master and his family loved them. And those deluded souls were more dangerous than the venal ones.

"Who do you worry about most?" Kenner asked.

Charles named three from his own plantation. "And at Trépagnier's, Dominique."

"Down here, we'll watch Bazile at the Meuillion place. He's half Indian, seems to like being one of the master's pets. But you never know. I've seen the worst toady up at the big house spit in the master's coffee."

"When they see us marching down the river road, they'll join us," Charles promised. "We'll be hundreds before we reach New Orleans."

The next morning, Charles left with a sack lunch from the kitchen and was in New Orleans by early afternoon. After he stabled the mule and the wagon, he ambled down Esplanade toward the fort, his hands in his pockets, a man who seemed to have nothing on his mind. The fort was abuzz with soldiers coming and going. There were rumors of trouble in the Spanish West Florida territory. Could be that Governor Claiborn would send his troops to counter the unrest east of Louisiana, but that was more than Charles could hope for. And the timing would have to be right. No, he couldn't count on the troops being absent from New Orleans.

He'd need a count of the soldiers in town. Chapin would have that, and more besides. Of the 25,000 souls in the city, 11,000 were slaves. Thousands would join them, but they would need arms when they rose up to prepare the city for the upriver rebels, and Chapin would know where they were and how to get them.

New Orleans in the summertime was a noxious place, the streets a mire of horse dung, the gutters clogged with the carcasses of dogs and rats, the river itself a stinking sewer. But this time of year, it was far more tolerable, and endlessly interesting. Filigreed balconies graced the streets, flowers bloomed in every courtyard even in December, and here and there he came upon an exotic bird in a bamboo cage, its yellow eye following him as he passed.

The streets were full of Sunday afternoon strollers come to town, ready to enjoy the fruits of all the labor that went into growing and tending and cutting and boiling the cane into the sugar that paid for their carriages and jewels. Gentlemen with rounded bellies strolled with their ladies on their arms, ladies clad in gowns that cost enough to feed a family of ten for a year.

And amid these fine glittering folk were the shabbily dressed multitude who curried the horses, cooked the meals, cleaned the privies. Charles eyed these dark-skinned New Orleanians as he walked the streets. How many of them would rise up when they learned their brethren upriver were coming in force to liberate them? A stout black fellow carrying a load of kindling on his back came toward him. Was he cowed and beaten down for all his brawn? It was hard to know what was in a man's heart when he had learned to make his face as bland as a milk cow's.

Among all these people, white, black, and every shade between, Charles felt himself invisible. No one here knew he was a slave driver, despised by his fellow slaves as a traitor to their race, wielding the whip for the white master, pushing the hands to work harder and faster and longer, year after year, until all the strength had been sucked from them. No one here even knew he was a slave.

He looked no different from the skilled workers who kept their earnings for themselves. Here in the city, nearly half of the black men and women were freed. Most of them were lighter-skinned like Charles, products of the union of white masters and black slaves. Some of those unions were founded on affection, and generous men had freed their children. Other slaves, skilled in carpentry or masonry or smithing, had belonged to masters who hired them out and allowed them to eventually buy their own freedom.

Charles's father had not freed him, but he had allowed him to learn to read. Charles's mother had wheedled that out of the old man, at least, and that was an accomplishment on her part. Because he was literate, Charles could earn a little money here and there. Andry allowed him a couple of bushels of nuts to sell, of corn or whatever was in season. He lent Charles to neighbors who needed some help with accounts or errands into town, even sometimes with writing messages in Charles's fine handwriting. He often pocketed a coin or two as a tip for those services.

So Charles walked the streets of New Orleans, and no one knew whether he were freed or enslaved, whether his pockets were full or empty. He felt liberated, anonymous, unbound by expectations and assumptions. A giddy elation crept into his soul, a sense of possibility and adventure.

He stopped a woman pulling a cart with a barrel of water. Fresh Spring Water, her sign said. Had she written it herself? Her clothes were worn but clean and mended. Her back was strong, pulling that heavy cart, her skin as light as his. Was she a free woman? Would the freed men and women support them when they took New Orleans?

"I'll take a cup," he said and offered her a coin.

She lifted the lid off her barrel and handed him a ladle. He hoped she hadn't filled her barrel with river water. He'd as soon drink from the pig trough.

He sipped the cold water. "It's good. Where'd it come from?"

"Bayou John," she said.

He eyed her over the cup. No placid cow, this one. Her look was sharp, her eyes judging him as he judged her.

"What you want?" she said.

He knew how to smile when he needed to. He raised the cup. "A drink of good water."

Her gaze sharpened. An intelligent woman. "Why you look at me like that?" she said.

He could tell her he always looked at pretty women. She was comely enough for that to ring true. Instead he looked around.

Foot traffic passed them by, paying them no mind. He turned back to her and eyed her headdress.

In a vain effort to save their husbands from temptation, jealous white ladies had insisted that the alluring, raven-haired mulattos should cover their hair. Clever, resilient, and inventive in their compliance, and no less alluring for it, freed women wore elaborate, fancifully folded tignons on their heads. The water seller's head covering was a simple, smooth calico wrapped tightly over her hair. Not the proud headdress of a freed woman.

"You're a slave," he said.

She regarded him with suspicion. He could see the thoughts flitting across her expressive face. Maybe he was one of those men who trapped women into being whores in their brothels. Maybe he was a kidnapper who stole black people, slaves or free, and then sold them upriver.

"Who are you?" she said.

"My name's Charles Deslondes. Belong to Manuel Andry."

"You not free either then," she said.

"No. Not yet." It was madness, what he'd just said. That last phrase, "not yet," was dangerous talk, and he'd let it slip from his lips.

She might have ended it there, but her black eyes bore into him.

"That's right," she said softly. "Not yet."

"What's your name?"

Suspicion returned. He could tell her mistress she'd been talking about freedom and get her whipped. Finally, she decided.

"Evangeline."

Charles handed her the ladle. "I expect I'll see you again, Evangeline."

She lowered her eyes as she touched his hand. "Be careful," she whispered.

He walked on, bolstered by the encounter. There was a woman who dreamed. There was a woman who was ready. There would be others.

Dark falling early this time of year, the gathering in Congo Square was well underway by mid-afternoon. Charles paused on the periphery, taking it all in. Every shade of skin milled about between vendors selling cheap rum or home-made whistles and pipes. A woman in a scarlet turban read the palm of a beautiful light-skinned woman dressed too well to be a slave. Maybe she was a courtesan. Another seer dressed all in black dealt tarot cards for a white man who hoped she would reveal a bright and prosperous future.

These town slaves, he noticed, had rounded limbs and an easy gait. They were not so worn down as the field slaves on the plantations. House slaves labored, but they did not labor in the wind and sun, the cold and rain, bent over and made old by relentless toil. Many of them understood their lives here in town were of relative ease. Many of them would be reluctant to join a rebellion. But not all of them. Some of these New Orleans slaves, like many on the plantations, had been brought here when their masters fled the uprisings in Haiti. They knew the heady promise of *liberté, égalité, fraternité*. They knew that freedom could be taken.

Two little girls, maybe ten years old, jostled him as they ran by, full of giggles and high spirits. There was joy here, in this place, at this moment. Smiling faces, laughter, even hilarity surrounded him, yet he stood aside. It was his habit, living as he did in a solitary world between his fellow slaves and the white master, but life was short, perhaps very short, for him. He was a fool to close himself off from every bright moment.

Stop thinking, he told himself. Enjoy life. He bought a cup of rum and winced as the first swallow went down. His belly burning from the harsh fire, he wound his way through the crowd and was once again at the palm reader's blanket.

"Come, *cher*. I tell you future for you." The woman in the red turban held out her braceleted arm, beckoning him. "Come to Mama Monique, I tell you how many sweet things gone warm your bed before you let some lucky girl catch you."

Her round open face, lighter than his own, smiled at him, including him in the charade. She waggled her fingers at him, then patted the blanket beside her.

Why not? Charles handed her a coin then lowered himself to sit cross-legged beside her.

"Pretty man like you, what you doing here all by you self? You let me have that fine hand you got there, and I tell you where you gone find you true love." She winked at him. "Maybe you find her right here."

He gave her his hand, palm up, and she traced her finger over the lines and creases. "Oh ho! You already find you true love. No? Yes! I see it here."

Charles grinned at her, amused, and she stroked his palm before she opened it up to gaze again. She grew quiet and still. All the fun left her face as she looked into his eyes.

She carefully closed his fingers over his palm. "God go with you," she said, and turned from him.

What had she seen? Disquieted, Charles moved into the crowd. It was all nonsense, wasn't it? He shrugged it off, determined not to lose the little slice of pleasure to be found here in Congo Square. Another cup of rum, that's what he wanted.

Darkness fell as he drained his second cup, and the drums started up. Even Charles, stiffened by a life of hiding, felt his blood stir. This was not drumming as communication. This was pure defiant joy, a celebration of *being*. Even a slave felt the blood pulse through his veins, felt his body respond to sun, sky, water, earth. To possibility.

He drew nearer, the reverberations pounding against his breast bone. Men danced in a circle, each moving independently, idiosyncratically. Shirtless, their bodies glowed with sweat on this cold December evening as they twirled and gyrated and stomped their feet to the rhythm. Charles closed his eyes and imagined himself stripped as they were. No shirt. No inhibitions. Wasn't that a kind of freedom? He ached for release from the burdens of secrecy, from the constraints of the mask he wore day in and day out. Wasn't he too a creature of heart and body, of yearning?

The drums pulsed through his flesh and into his bones. He shrugged off his jacket and pulled his shirt over his head, letting them drop at his feet. Shuffling, he entered the circle with his eyes half-closed, yielding himself to the driving beat.

Torches flickered around the dancers, the women weaving their line around and through the circle of men. The drums echoed through the night, pounding and pummeling, drowning out all thought and even sense. Charles became only body, his mind given over entirely to the overwhelming thunder of the drums.

Women tore off their head coverings letting their hair flow wild and free. They slipped out of their tops, some shed their skirts and danced nude in wild, sensual abandon.

The drums pounded and thrummed through him, transforming him into an elemental being, purely sensation, purely male. A bare-breasted woman, skin as dark as the night, shimmied her body up close to him. She ran her hands over his ribs. She stepped closer yet and ground her hips into his, pressing her breasts against him as the drums drove them past reason and thought into deep, primitive realms.

She led him into the deep shadows of the park where he took her, their bodies grinding and pumping with the throbbing, pulsing drums. They climaxed together in cataclysmic release, but she was desperate for more and more, her fingers digging into his flesh, prodding and urging as her hips pumped beneath him. He caught up with her and they heaved against each other, wild and frantic, his every thrust carrying her with him into a throbbing, mindless exhilaration. Their moment, when it came, was explosive, searing, shattering. Charles stiffened and shuddered, his mind gone, his body drained.

Panting, exhausted, he rolled off and reached for her. She pressed her mouth to his, then slid out of his arms and fled into the night.

He lay there on the cold ground, in the dark, listening to the drums. God, he thought, but his mind could go no further. He closed his eyes and let the pounding rhythms wash over him and through him. He was the earth, he was the pulsing beat. He was blood and sinew and muscle. He was man. For now, it was enough.

At midnight, Charles made his way through the quiet streets to a small dark house in Tremé. If neighbors should see him or hear his faint knock on the door, they would never tell. Tremé was made up of free blacks and refugees from the rebellions in the Caribbean. Even slaves lived here on their masters' sufferance.

Charles shivered waiting for the door to open. He'd gone back for his shirt and jacket, but found only the shirt, stomped into the dirt, grimy and gritty. The door opened just enough for Charles to step inside. Once the door was closed behind him, a candle flamed into life.

Chapin looked him over. "What happened to you? You look like you been run over by a herd of horses."

Charles fingered the dirty shirt, remembering the woman's hands hot on his skin.

"Here, let me have that." Chapin's woman climbed off the bed. "Maybe I'll get enough dirt out of it to plant me a patch of collards."

"Thank you, Mary." Charles shucked off the shirt and went to the fireplace to warm his hands over the glowing coals.

"You hungry?" Mary asked.

"Don't trouble. I'll get something in the morning."

"Seems like a man in my house half-naked, he ought to get hisself fed. Sit down. I got some sweet potatoes and a little cornbread left."

Mary set a tin plate in front of him. In the flickering light, he cut into the deep orange of a fat sweet potato, lifted a big bite to his mouth, then sighed. "Mary, that's the best tater I ever ate."

Chapin sat across from him, the candle light casting gruesome shadows over his face. "How is it upriver?"

Charles told him what he knew, where they were strongest, where they were weakest. "Kenner and the rest are waiting for me to bring word of what's going on here. What do you know about West Florida? Claiborn likely to get involved?"

Chapin watched his wife brushing the dirt off Charles' cotton shirt. "Boss man says Claiborn's an ass. No, he says he's an arrogant ass, but none of the French like the Americans. Especially not the governor." He ran a hand over his short wiry hair. "Could be he'll send troops in, but we can't count on it."

"He got enough men to make a difference in Spanish Florida?"

"Got some volunteer militias might go when he calls. Got a small troop garrisoned here in town. A few sailors out on the river if the commodore is willing to let them on land. And the dragoons."

Charles nodded. The dragoons were crack soldiers. It would be a bloody battle to take New Orleans with the dragoons defending it. But if Claiborn sent them to subdue Spanish West Florida, Charles and his rebels would own the city.

"Here, put your shirt on. That's the best I can do without putting it in the wash pot."

Charles accepted the shirt from Mary and slipped it over his head. "You did a fine job. Thank you, Mary."

"Mary, get him that top blanket off the bed. Charles, you stay here by the fire tonight and I'll take you by the fort in the morning, then on down to the barracks. Get you a feel for the number Claiborn has in town."

Charles lay on the bare floor wrapped in the threadbare quilt. He usually had to make himself clear his mind or he'd be up all night thinking, planning, worrying. But not tonight. He was asleep before he'd heaved a second breath.

In the early morning, after Mary fed them eggs and biscuits, Charles and Chapin crossed through the Vieux Carre and down Magazine Street to the parade grounds where the dragoons were already gathered in the light fog. Plenty of admiring ladies and envious young men stood around the perimeter, impressed with the manly cut of their uniforms or the masterly precision of their drills. Charles was particularly interested in the musketry practice. The crack shooters arranged themselves in three rows. The first row fired, knelt to reload, the second row fired, then knelt. By the time the third row had fired, the first was up and ready again.

Charles's familiarity with his old air gun did not prepare him for the accuracy and speed of the dragoons' muskets. He doubted the militia weapons cached in Andry's armory matched these guns, but the principles and procedures would be the same.

Pan, cartridge, prime, load, ram. Then hoist the long gun to the shoulder, take aim, and fire. Again, and again, until each row of shooters fired in unison, opened the cartridge, fed the powder and then the ball, primed, loaded, rammed the rod down the barrel. Hoisted to the shoulder, aimed, fired.

He would have to teach his men how to handle the muskets. Without their having a musket to practice on. They'd wouldn't get their hands on the actual firearms until the night they broke into the armory, until the night they declared to the world, freedom is mine!

He would teach them. They would do what they could. They had numbers on their side, and heart, and justice. They would own this territory when the smoke cleared.

He spent another hour with Chapin observing the fort at the other end of the levy, tallying as close as they could figure how many soldiers guarded New Orleans. The rebels would outnumber them easy. Then Charles said goodbye to Chapin, strode back through town, and bought a used jacket down at the levy where the vendors vied for space with the stevedores.

On Rue Chartres, a bookseller swept his front stoop, a sign freshly painted in green and gold swinging over his head. Through the window Charles could see hundreds of books lined up on shelves. He yearned to go inside and run his fingers along the spines of all those books. What could be in so many books? Philosophy, of course. Stories. Mathematics? Men did more with numbers than add and subtract, multiply and divide. He'd seen a surveyor once doing calculations that mystified him. And more, so much more in that little store.

But the bookseller would never let a man like him inside, not if he knew he was a slave. If a slave had somehow learned to read, he'd best keep it to himself. Someday, though, he would walk into this bookstore and claim it for himself and all his people. Maybe he would be a bookseller himself, and he'd teach men, women, and children to read, as many of them as came to him and wanted to learn.

But that time was not yet come. He turned down Bienville to fulfill his errand for Mr. Andry. As he approached the slave market, the stench of despair and filth from the holding pen rose over the stockade fence. Further along, he dipped his head to step through the low arch into the showroom and found another odor altogether. His gut clenched at the slave women lined up against the wall where they endured the indifferent eyes of white women and the calculating eyes of white men. The room reeked of fear.

He settled himself by examining the chalk board's list of bargains. Three blacksmiths on sale. A seamstress trained in Parisian millinery, a maid skilled at hairdressing. He didn't need a blacksmith or a fancy woman's attendant. He was here for a field hand and a cook.

Dressed in his homespun trousers and canvas jacket, Charles crossed his arms and watched the other buyers. A portly woman attended by a stalwart black man wore a blue silk dress and a fur ruff. He didn't know anything about furs, but it looked expensive. Her slave, a man black as Africa, stood proudly at her elbow in a suit of black linen, far finer than anything Charles had ever donned. Fool. Did he think his finery made him any less the monkey to his fat white woman?

He ran his eye over the women for sale. "House," the hand-printed sign on one woman's chest read. "Field," on another. A man in a top hat used his cane to lift the field hand's skirt, a little higher, a little higher, teasing the girl with how slowly he exposed her. The girl's knees and hands trembled, and Charles turned away, his chest tightening. She'd better toughen up if she meant to survive.

At the end of the row, he found two women with "Cook" on their placards. The first woman was a beauty. She stood tall and erect, and she knew enough to keep her eyes on the buyers' knees, but fear was all over her. She'd be easy pickings for Manuel Andry, who would use her then pass her on to his son. He settled on the slight woman whose chest was too flat, whose lips too thick to entice. Maybe.

Charles nodded to a broker and then handed him a slip of paper with the price he was willing to pay and the number on the cook's placard. He threaded his way through the other buyers, avoiding touching, avoiding eye-contact. At the row of field hands, he did as the well-dressed planters did. He walked slowly along, taking an overview of size and shape and muscle tone. He watched other buyers squeeze a man's biceps or peer into his mouth. Bile rose in his throat at the sight of a tall, muscled black man dropping his trousers at the buyer's request to see his manhood. He stopped, waiting to see what passed over the slave's face. Humiliation and shame and defeat, that's what Charles read. He'd make a good hand, a good breeder. Not what Charles was looking for.

"You got the very devil in your eye, boy." A corpulent buyer had his cane under a slave's chin, forcing it up. "Nothing but trouble, I wager. Let's see your back."

A broker stepped forward. "Take a look at this fellow's thighs. Feel that arm. He's worth any two ordinary field hands."

The slave mastered his face and stared at the far wall.

The buyer cocked his head, unconvinced. "Let's get the shirt off."

The broker thumped the slave on the shoulder. The slave pulled his shirt over his head. "Look at the musculature on this boy's abdomen. Don't see that very often. Strong as an ox."

"Turn him around."

With a defeated sigh, the broker pushed at the slave to turn, revealing a back knotted with scar tissue.

"Just as I thought," the fat man said. "A trouble maker. You'll make no sale to me with a demon like this one. What do you mean offering such trouble to decent owners, I want to know."

Charles waited for the slave to turn back, waited to see what was in his eyes. Nothing. Not a glimmer of anger, not a hint of hate simmering behind the far-away stare. When the broker and the buyer moved on, Charles stepped close.

"What's your name, *boy?*" Charles said, dosing the last word with spite.

There it was, the merest flicker of fire in the man's eyes. And then the eyes went blank, the gaze vacant. Fire, and control. Good.

"Justice. Sir."

"Where'd you get a name like that? Your master call you Justice?"

The slave didn't answer, didn't look at him.

"You gave it to yourself, is that it?"

Charles weighed the risks. He'd have to be on his guard every minute of the two days' travel back to Andry's. The fellow outweighed him, and he'd be looking for his chance. But he might be useful.

Charles motioned to the broker, who handed him a form. Charles wrote in the slave's number and a low bid. The broker spat in disgust when he read the figure.

"The boy's trouble," Charles reminded him.

"All right," he growled. "He's yours."

Charles glanced at the *boy* standing there, half a head taller than he was. The boy's eye skittered over Charles's face then quickly resumed an unfocused gaze at the opposite wall.

He left his human purchases in the holding. He had one more task, and strode to the levy where vendors had laid out their wares. If Annique were with him, he'd buy her a bunch of white violets from the little girl surrounded by bouquets. They'd stroll through the crowd and listen to the strange languages the sailors spoke, or clap to the music of minstrels with their banjos and flutes. As it was, he could at least take her something.

Two proud, glamorous quadroon women sashayed by him, exotic as scarlet birds. Likely they were plaçeés, rich white men's mistresses, both of them in fine dresses, both of them in the height of fashion with their soaring, elaborate tignons.

That's what he'd take home to Annique. The head coverings were pretty, but they were something more than that. A symbol of individuality and resistance.

At the calico stall, his eye was caught by a print of blues and reds swirling around purple starbursts. He could see himself and Annique discovering how to tie the cloth into the fanciest tignon in the parish. He would be her mirror, and she would hold her head just so with that impish gleam in her eye. He blinked. With sudden revelation, he realized he missed her. Not just Annique in her bed, but Annique who teased and laughed, who was content to be quiet with him, who knew him.

Charles Deslondes, who never attached himself to anyone, very much wanted to be back with Annique in her little cabin under the chinaberry tree. Bemused, he fingered the length of calico, Annique's calico, until he remembered he had miles to cover that day.

The swatch of cloth tucked in a pocket, Charles reclaimed the wagon and mule, then collected his purchases. Lydia, the new cook, climbed in the wagon like a lamb. Justice stood immobile behind it, the dread coming off him in waves. Charles waited him out till finally Justice heaved his butt on the wagon and swung himself aboard, chains and all.

One chain around Lydia's wrist then through a grommet on the wagon's floor was plenty for her. For Justice, Charles ran three. He drove them through the busy streets and onto the river road. At noon, Charles stopped in a shady patch on the side of the road and fed Andry's new chattel.

They ate silently, Justice sullen, Lydia relaxed. Charles figured for her, the worst was over, the standing and waiting while white people poked and stared and treated her like a thing. Now, she was to be a cook's helper, not a field hand, cause enough to let go of all her tension.

A bluebird lit on the back board. Charles held his breath, filling up on blue, a blue so blue he could taste it. The mule flicked its tail at flies and the bird flew off.

"That's a good sign, a bluebird," Lydia said. "It mean good things to come."

"It's just a pretty bird," Charles said.

"Master, you got a lot of slaves at your place?"

"I'm not your master. You belong to Manuel Andry." He corked the jug and gave Lydia a look. "And so do I." He fished the key to unlock her chain out of his pocket. "I let you do your business behind that tree over there, am I going to have to come looking for you?"

"No, sir. I ain't a runner."

He unhooked her chain from the wagon bed and watched her drag it through the dust. Then he turned to Justice. "They got swamps where you come from?"

"Yeah, I seen swamps."

There were slaves who knew the swamps and all its dangers, and still ran into them, wild to be free of the unrelenting labor, the white man's boot, the hopelessness. Charles understood, but he called them fools. Unless he found them before some gator or snake got them, they dragged themselves back to the quarters sick, swollen up from mosquito bites, and starving. The half dozen times he'd recovered a runaway, he'd given the man a few days to heal, gave him a whipping, then found he had a pretty good worker for a year or so, maybe for the rest of his life. It took the starch out of a man, a few days running through the swamps half mad with bites and risk and fear.

He'd heard the overseer on the Latiffe plantation got a kick out of letting the dogs tear into his runaways, but Charles didn't use dogs. He'd been a boy when he saw what a pack could do to a man. Years later, he still sometimes woke in the night sick with fear, the dream of being chased and torn apart by a pack of dogs as real as the sheen of sweat on his brow.

"You ever seen an alligator?" he asked the new man.

Justice shrugged, his jaw set. Looked to Charles like he was unconvinced the swamp was a bad bet. He left him chained in the wagon. He could wet himself if he had to go.

At dusk, Charles drove into the side lane of the Volker plantation and pulled up at the overseer's cabin to make arrangements for Lydia and Justice to spend the night in the lock-up. While the overseer's wife made him up a cold supper to eat on the porch, Charles made a point of making friends of the lean hounds lying around the yard.

Later he climbed into the barn's loft and bedded down in sweet hay. The moon rose, painting the land in silver. Lights in the overseer's cabin had been long out, not a glimmer of fire or candle in the windows.

Charles slipped down from the loft and into the night. As he glided through the shadows of the peach orchard, two of the hounds picked up his scent and loped after him. He stopped and scratched behind their ears. One of them licked his hand, and the two were satisfied. They followed along in silent companionship as

45

Charles strode toward the far end of the slave row. At the last cabin, a door opened just enough to let him in.

Chapter Six

"I tole Kook don't eat them old greens, they was going to the hogs, but he too hungry to wait for the corn bread and now he got a belly full of hurt." Though Rosie didn't look at the man, she leaned on her hoe, looking relaxed and guileless as she ran on, like she and the overseer were having a friendly chat. "Guess he listen to his woman next time, yessir."

"I'm not feeding a slacker to squat in the bushes all day. Tell him to get out here and get to work."

"Yes, sir, Mr. Crawley, soon as he can. But he got the squirts and you know we women don't want to see none of that out here in the field where we working and stepping." She shook her head at the certainty of that fact. "No sir, we don't want to see none of that."

The overseer rode on. Rosie exchanged a look with Quamana, then went back to her hoeing. Kook had been gone since just after Crawley had handed out hoes from the tool shed that morning. Half a day, and he had only just now missed him. That was good. Kook would be back by the time they handed their hoes in. He'd better be. Crawley kept careful count of his hoes and his hands.

Kook followed a path so faint he twice thought he'd lost it for sure. Back here behind the cultivated fields you had to watch your step. You'd be pacing along on dry ground among trees and bushes, and then would come a wet patch. He stepped carefully around those shallow puddles. Quick sand all out in these marshy woods.

He shivered, thinking about getting sucked into one of those pits, the wet sand closing in on him, swallowing his screams, filling his mouth, his eyes. Nobody would even find his bones until judgment day. And Rosie would never know what happened to him.

Rosie was the only woman to see past the pretty smiles he gave all the girls. She knew his heart. And he'd given it to her. Then Joshua was born, and Lila the next year. He loved them, sure he did. But it ate at him--he'd brought two more slaves into the world. He'd die willingly if it meant his babies wouldn't grow up to be mules in this life.

He'd been plodding north for hours and he still hadn't met any of the maroons out here. The community of escaped slaves knew these woods, and they were supposed to find him, not the other way around. A field nigger, that's what they called him, a field nigger didn't know how to move out here, they said. Their scouts would find him thrashing through the brush long before he found their camp in the thick woods south of Lake Maurepas. The way they told it, they numbered maybe sixty. They had babies born in the camp grown into men and women now.

Kook figured living out here was not easy. Mosquitoes, gators, fogs full of sickness. Not much in the way of tools except what they made themselves. But if they found a patch of ground dry enough to plant, most anything would grow. They could fish, hunt possum and gators. And they were free. The whites didn't come back in here to roust them out. They didn't want slaves who'd tasted what it felt like to be a man. They might infect the rest. And maybe the whites were scared of the maroons, too, because these people were not going back into slavery without a fight.

Kook moved through a patch of brush, not worried much about snakes on a cool day like this. He shoved aside a palmetto branch and there he was. A maroon. He bore deep slashes and dots of scar tissue on his face, scars like Kook's and Quamana's that proved he had once been an African warrior, a man. Only this maroon labored for himself and his own. He was still a man.

"You Quamana?"

He shook his head. "Kook."

"Come on, and watch your step. This is copperhead country."

They came to a clearing where a possum roasted on a spit over the fire. Two men stood as they approached. The eldest must have been six foot five, the others no doubt his sons with the same long limbs.

"Big Tom," Kook said.

"Quamana didn't come?"

Kook shook his head. "Can't talk his way out of trouble any better than a four year old, and the overseer's got it in for him.

He'd never get away with being gone a whole day. Me?" Kook flashed one of his ingratiating smiles. "Everybody loves a happy slave."

"Come to the fire. Sit."

They offered him sweet water from a jug and shared the possum. Kook relayed the news from New Orleans, how many soldiers, how many slaves.

"Nothing easy 'bout New Orleans," Big Tom said.

"That where you come from?"

"Where I run from. You got a city full of slaves, sure. But they got it good in town. How many willing to risk their lives for all you field niggers?"

"You must not have thought you had it so good. You ran."

Big Tom touched the ritual scars across his chest. "I knew what it was like to be a man. They don't know nothing but being a slave."

"How many you think will join us?"

"Maybe two, maybe three out of ten."

Kook stared at the fire, discouraged. They needed more than that to secure the city.

"It'll be enough," Big Tom's son said. "All the scared ones got to do is stay out of the way. When it's done, they'll come to us."

"Some of them will pick up a blade and fight for the whites," Kook muttered.

"Then we gone have to kill some of our own. They make a choice, they live or die by it."

Kook studied Big Tom's face. The scarring made him fierce, but the black eyes were far more menacing. This was a man ready to kill.

"You and your sons are free out here. What's this rebellion to you?"

The smile that split his heavy dark lips did not diminish the threat in his eyes. "My woman wants a floor under her feet. She wants a glass window to look out of when it rains. She wants shoes on her children's feet." He nodded at his son. "That one there, he wants to read."

"What do you want?"

The big man looked around the tree-lined glade. "Sometimes these woods close in on a man. Another kind of prison. You have children?" Kook nodded. "Then you know what I want. I want my children to see the ocean, the mountains. I want them free to walk anywhere on this green earth."

"You could sit out here in the woods, safe. Join us when we've beat the whites down."

Big Tom snorted. "You got one chance, boy. You need us."

Kook nodded. "Yes. We do."

"And we need weapons."

"You'll have them."

"Where from?"

"Andry's place is the armory for the militia. Swords, firearms, uniforms, it's all there. We start at Andry's. You meet up with us there or on the road."

"When?"

"Soon."

The second son who had not yet spoken sneered. "I been hearing that all my life. Soon." The young man leaned forward. "*How* soon?"

"Not up to me."

"Quamana okay with this, the waiting? How long he willing to wait?"

Kook had played pacifier to Quamana over and again. Frustration and impatience would build up in his friend until he was a danger not only to himself but to all of them. If he let his anger erupt, the whole plantation would go up in flames. The very trees would become torches, the ponds would steam, the earth smolder. Such was Quamana's rage. Kook didn't know how much longer he could cool him down with Crawley tormenting him and the endless waiting for the word from Charles. It had to be soon.

"Quamana knows the time has to be right."

"Carnival a good time to rise up. The whites'll be half drunk until Lent."

Kook nodded. "We're ready. Just waiting for the word."

"The word from who?" the second son demanded.

Kook eyed him across the fire. "You know I can't tell you that."

"Leave him alone, Ezra. He'd be a fool letting out who's in on this. Even to you."

"You going to wander around out here looking for us when it's time? Crashing through the brush, hoping we find you before the fighting starts and it's all over?"

"You know the language of the drums."

"Some of it," Big Tom said.

Kook had practiced for this. There was no drum at hand, and he had to show them what to listen for. He bent his knee and tightened his thigh. Using his fingers and palms, he drummed the message that would tell them the time had come.

The whites had heard the drums all their lives. They thought the slaves amused themselves, their primitive blood soothed by the repetition of beats, by the semi-trances they induced. The whites were deaf to the variations of tone, the repetition of phrases, the meaning of changes in rhythm and pace. And the reverberations of a corps of drummers carried for miles, to be picked up by other drummers and transmitted down the river and deep into the woods. The maroons would know within minutes of Charles sending the signal out.

Kook checked the sun through the forest canopy. He had to be back before dusk, long before, if he didn't want Crawley to miss him. Rosie could only fool him so long before the man, dull-witted as he was, suspected he'd snuck off. Maybe he'd take it out on Rosie, but probably not. Rosie had the gift, could make a man believe the rain showered down in drops of honey if she gave it half a try.

"How many of you can we count on?" Kook asked.

Big Tom looked at his sons, then back at Kook. He held up his hands, ten fingers, then ten fingers again.

Kook inhaled. Twenty men who knew their own minds. They'd be a formidable addition. "I'll tell them."

He left them in the glade and moved through the brush as quickly as he could, wary of copperheads and sand pits and poison oak.

Maybe he should lead Rosie and the children out here to stay with Big Tom's clan before the violence started. They'd be safe. They'd have their freedom, or a measure of it. Because their chances of winning this rebellion were no better than fifty-fifty. Maybe he was fooling himself. Maybe the odds were not that good. But they had done it in Haiti. And Charles, Harry Kenner, Quamana and he had been thorough. And careful.

They'd planned. They'd recruited with every caution. A man brought in another man only if he knew him down to the particles in his blood, down to the dreams running through his head. When they could, they relied on slaves who'd come from the same tribes in Africa and spoke the same language. Trust had to be earned, the fire in the belly had to be stoked. Too many slaves had made peace with their fate. They were no good to them, men like that. They needed men ready to kill, and to die.

They had done all they could do. They had taught their men the drill--pan, cartridge, prime, load, ram, fire--had practiced in pantomime over and over, the best they could do until they had the weapons in their hands. They were ready. What was Charles waiting for? Kook couldn't doubt the man's commitment. Respected his cunning and ability to organize and strategize. But what did he wait for?

Dark came early this time of year. Kook hurried back, eager to be with Rosie and the children, snug in their little cabin before the sun set. He came through the outer cane fields, cleared now, ready for the next planting, and strode through the cold, moist dirt. As he approached the quarters, he slowed his pace. He was supposed to be sick with the bellyache.

The evening bell rang out, Crawley calling the field hands in to the shed to turn in their hoes. A few weeks ago, at the end of harvest, they'd turned in their cane knives, their machetes, their strippers. This shed would be their first stop when the word came. They'd break in and take every weapon, two or three to a man if there were enough.

Kook retrieved the hoe he'd hidden that morning and joined the hands shuffling by Crawley. When he approached the overseer, he slouched and put on a face of misery.

"You decided to show up, huh?" Crawley sneered at him. "You think you gone get a day's rations for laying out all day, you got it wrong, boy. Lessen you take the food off your babies' plates, you gone do without tonight, you hear?"

"I don't want nothing, Mr. Crawley. I's sick as a dog."

Rosie appeared at his shoulder. "I tole him not to eat them collard greens, didn't I? I tole him to get on outta here so I didn't have to smell his stink, but he come back, just like I told you, Mr. Crawley. I gone take him on home now, and he be better tomorrow. You'll see, Mr. Crawley. Right as rain tomorrow."

Rosie had him by the arm and tugged him away, her mouth still chattering. Anybody didn't know better, they'd think she was as empty-headed as Kook pretended to be. They were safer that way, had stayed out from under the overseer's whip these last years.

But he didn't want his son growing up wearing the same mask, acting the fool. He wanted a son to be able to stand tall and walk through the world with dignity. A man like Quamana, but free.

After the candles had all been snuffed in the quarters, Quamana slipped in through the back door. Kook sat with him before the low fire, comfortable sitting Indian style, his hands loose on his knees. His friend's body betrayed the constant tension he lived with, every muscle taut, his skin tight across his face, his lips a straight hard line.

Kook told him they could expect twenty maroons. They'd bring their knives, but they wanted weapons.

"We'll have plenty."

"And they want to know when. They want it to be now."

Quamana said nothing. He stared into the fire.

"What is he waiting for?"

Quamana shook his head. "I don't know."

Kook hesitated before he said what he knew others must be thinking. "What if we went ahead without Charles?"

Quamana raised his head with a start. "No. Charles is the key to this. Without him, word would have leaked out, and the whites would have us all in chains. Or our heads on pikes. He's the one knows all the reins to gather, all along the river. Without him–"

He hadn't heard Quamana string that many words together in months. Kook held up his hand. "Yes. You're right. But talk to him, Quamana. People are getting tired of waiting."

"I'll talk to him."

Kook glanced over at Rosie's body mounded under the old quilt on the bed. She had listened to their talk for a while, but exhaustion claimed her. She slept now.

"Quamana," he said, his voice low. "Something happens to me, you take Rosie and the kids. Take care of them. Make them your own."

Quamana shook his head. "Whatever happens to you will happen to me, too."

They sat in the dark, thinking ahead. It was going to be ugly, winning this war. There would be blood. And if they failed, there would be retribution.

"Take her and the children to the maroons," Quamana said.

"I don't know if she'll go."

After a moment, Quamana rose, touched Kook's shoulder, and let himself out into the night.

Kook sat a while. He was ready to die. Had been for a long time, if he could die as a warrior, fighting for his freedom. Living like this, no more than another mule on the plantation – not a life for a man. And it was worth dying if it meant his babies wouldn't grow up to be mules too.

He got up, his knees creaking. He was only twenty, but the incessant work, the heat, the cold, the short rations – he felt the weight of age, the weight of worry. He bent over little Lila, her arms and legs spread out like a puppy offering her belly, confident she was safe and loved. He pulled the cover back over his baby girl. Joshua, a big boy now, still slept with his thumb in his mouth, his other hand fisted under his chin. His Joshua didn't miss much. He watched the overseer striding past the cabins with the whip in his hand and felt the tension in his mama when Crawley came close. How long would it be before Lila too slept with her hands fisted?

When the day came, there would be violence, fear, and blood, black and white. And if the whites beat them back, there would be vengeance. No telling what horrors they'd do to his wife and children when they counted up the white men Kook had killed, when they learned happy, smiling, shuffling Kook had been plotting all these months.

He'd insist. Rosie and the children would be safely among the maroons before the fighting started.

Chapter Seven

The next morning, Quamana stood in his usual posture with arms crossed over his chest and his feet spread as Crawley assigned the work gangs to their tasks. Quamana was tired of hoeing rows across the damp dark fields. Maybe Crawley would make up a detail to clean out that drainage ditch. Getting so overgrown the snakes had made a home of it.

And maybe he and Kook would be sent with rakes and machetes to hack out the growth and eliminate the critters. Last time, a snake had slithered over Kook's foot and he'd squealed like a little girl. Quamana smiled. Could be a good day.

"Where's Quamana?" Crawley said.

Since Quamana stood a head taller than everyone on the place except Kook, who was only a half-finger shorter, and since he was standing not ten feet away from Crawley, he didn't bother to answer.

"I said where's Quamana?" Crawley snapped, deliberately looking beyond him.

Kook nudged him. "Not worth it," he murmured.

Quamana sighed. He raised his hand.

"You and Bo give Smithy a hand today," Crawley said, still acting like it wasn't worth his while to actually look at Quamana. Did the man think he hurt Quamana's feelings by not looking at him? All Crawley did was prove he had something to prove. Quamana suppressed a smirk. In the Asante kingdom across the ocean, the overseer would be left at home with the women when it was time to go to war.

The slaves broke to go about their work. Bo fell into step next to Quamana on the way to the blacksmith shop. Bo was in his prime, strong and quiet. He'd run for freedom more than once judging from the scars on his back and his mutilated ear. A worthy man. Quamana knew Kook had recruited him into the rebel forces, but secrecy was so well-enforced, Bo knew nothing of other recruits, not even of Quamana's involvement. So they crossed the yard to the shop in comfortable silence.

Smithy walked with them to the carpentry shop where the massive new cane cart was waiting for its wheels. Quamana and Bo would provide the muscle while Smithy and Pierre, the carpenter, finessed the wheels onto the axles.

The first wheel, hub and axle both generously greased, went on smooth and easy. The men moved around to the other side and got to work on the second wheel.

Bo and Quamana steadied and supported the undercarriage, the improvised jack between them, Smithy underneath for the fitting. Maybe they had grease on their hands, or maybe the jack slipped. The wagon shifted, its weight quickly sliding down into Bo's arms and hands. He shouted, he bent his knees into it, trying to catch the bulk before it crashed down on Smithy.

Quamana leapt to balance the weight, shoving up while Smithy scrambled out of the way, but the wagon toppled off the jack and neither he nor Bo could stop its momentum. Smithy was clear. Pierre was clear. Quamana leapt out of the way, but Bo stumbled as the wagon crashed down.

Bo screamed. He lay in the dirt, his foot caught, his ankle twisted under the wagon.

Quamana and Smithy heaved the weight off him while Pierre dragged Bo clear. He was still screaming when he caught sight of his twisted foot and passed out.

For a long moment the three men simply stared at Bo's foot and ankle. There wasn't anybody going to be able to make that right.

"You're bleeding," Pierre said, gesturing at Quamana's arm.

Quamana looked down, surprised. There was a gash on his upper arm. The blood dripped off his fingertips. He shook his hand to rid it of blood drops. "Let's move him while he's still out."

Pierre ran for Crawley. Quamana and Smithy carried Bo to his cabin and lay him on his cot. Mercifully, Bo hadn't wakened.

Crawley came in with Pierre right behind him. In the day-to-day running of the plantation, Crawley or sometimes his wife did the doctoring and patching up. The slaves preferred to make their own remedies, but if Crawley thought a slave wasn't mending fast enough, he'd intervene. He was fond of purgatives and emetics that left a body feeling weak and washed out, guaranteed to discourage malingering, so generally the slaves kept their ailments to themselves.

Bo's eyes flew open. He bit his lip to keep from screaming, but he couldn't stop the groan from deep in his gut. Quamana couldn't see how Bo could keep that foot. Couldn't see how he'd ever walk easy across the land again.

Crawley stared at Bo's ankle. Shook his head and stared some more. "That foot's going have to come off."

"No! No, no, no! No!"

Quamana bent over and squeezed Bo's shoulder, pushing him back down.

"I'll send for the doc." Crawley turned to leave.

Bo panted, and a thin keening crept past his lips.

"Mr. Crawley," Smithy said, "you got some of that laudanum? If he could have a little for the pain."

Crawley considered it. "All right. I'll send some down."

In a few minutes, Mrs. Crawley entered the cabin. She scowled like she didn't like what she smelled. She ignored the three men standing around Bo, uncapped the bottle of laudanum, and poured the elixir into a spoon.

"Open up," she said to Bo. Standing out from the bed so that she had to bend way over to reach him, she carefully spooned the laudanum into his mouth without touching him.

She started to put the spoon and the bottle back in her apron pocket, but Smithy said, "Miz Crawley, he hurt awful bad."

Bo's teeth were clamped tight, but he couldn't stop the trembling of his hands or the tears flowing over his cheeks.

With a little snort of disgust, Mrs. Crawley poured out another spoonful and fed it to Bo. Then she left the cabin without ever having looked at his foot.

That one human being could be so indifferent to another's suffering. Especially a woman. This, Quamana thought, is why we have to kill them. They're hardly human.

He knelt by the bed and gripped Bo's hand until the laudanum took him under. Pierre and Smithy went back to work. "Should a used a pulley and tackle," Pierre muttered on the way out.

Quamana built a fire, then pulled his bloody shirt off. He tore the clean sleeve and wrapped it around his arm above the gash to stop the bleeding. It had slowed, but it was annoying to have the constant drip off his fingers.

Then he sat and leaned against the bed frame to wait for the doctor. If the man took Bo's foot, Quamana would be needed to hold him down.

It was mid-afternoon when Quamana heard a horse and wagon pull into the lane between the cabins. Bo was awake, but dazed. The pain seemed to have moved away from his core. It was down the other end of the bed, in his confusion. A good thing, Quamana thought.

He went to the porch, but it wasn't the doc Crawley had brought back. It was a woman. A small woman. Quamana was disgusted. What good would a little thing like this white woman be with a saw in her hand? He was probably going to have to cut through the bone himself if Crawley didn't do it.

Old Serafina hurried across the lane, three little fellas in her wake. She'd been in and out all day, bringing water and at mid-day a cold dinner for Quamana. "Mr. Crawley," she called. "Mr. Crawley, where the doctor?"

That's what Quamana wanted to know, too, but only Serafina could get away with questioning the overseer.

"Now Serafina, you go on back inside with the little ones. This here is the doctor's kin and he's been training her to help out. She'll do right in there, so you go on."

A civil answer for once.

The little woman strode from the wagon to the cabin, climbed the few steps with purpose, gave Quamana a glance and brushed right by him. He followed her in and stood at Bo's bedside.

The woman took off her bonnet. She leaned over Bo's foot and peered. "Can you light the lantern, please?" she said to Quamana. He lit it and held it up for her. The light fell on her bare head. Her hair was full of fiery red. There had been a red-headed sailor on board the slave ship that brought Quamana across the ocean, but it had not shone like this with bars of gold and fire.

She looked a long time. Then she lightly skimmed her fingers over the tight, swollen skin. With a little more pressure, she felt the bones underneath. Bo gasped.

"The skin's not really broken. Just abraded," she murmured.

"All right, Miss Evie. I'll leave you to it. Quamana here will lend you a hand."

The lady doctor looked at Crawley, measuring him. Quamana figured she was going to need someone with grit to hold Bo down, whatever she did to his foot. Crawley just declared he was not that man. She looked at him as she might a worm and turned her back on him. Instead she studied Quamana. He returned her steady gaze.

She nodded once. "Very well, Mr. Crawley. You may leave."

Quamana almost laughed. This woman, no higher than his biceps, had put the overseer in his place.

She rummaged in her worn leather bag. On it, in faded scratched gold, was a staff with two snakes twined around it. An odd design for a woman, Quamana thought. From the bag, she produced a bottle, a spoon, and a stick. "What's your name?" she asked her patient.

"I'm Bo."

"Swallow this down, Bo." She spooned a tonic into his mouth that smelled the same as the laudanum Mrs. Crawley had given him that morning.

"The stick's for you to bite. This is going to hurt. But I'll wait a few minutes for you to get dopey. Maybe you won't need the stick."

"Don't cut my foot off, Miss. Don't. Please don't cut my foot off!"

She crossed her arms over her chest. "It is not my intention to cut your foot off, Bo. Now lie back and close your eyes. You'll be asleep in a few minutes."

Quamana watched her stand like a silent sentinel as Bo's breathing steadied, then slowed. Her eyes glanced around the cabin, flitted over the bloody sleeve Quamana had tied around the gash in his arm, and back to Bo, watching his torpor deepen into sleep. She waited a few more minutes.

"Very well," she said. "I need the lantern held just here, if you please."

Quamana did as she asked. Then she set to work. Abandoning her gentle touch, she probed Bo's ankle and foot, seeing with her fingers just what had happened to the bones under the swollen flesh.

While she studied Bo, Quamana studied her. Here it was winter time, and the woman smelled like spring flowers. Her skin was pale as milk, and she was afflicted with light brown freckles, thousands of them, on her face and throat, on the backs of her hands. Her lips were thin, and her chin small. She was not beautiful, but her hair dazzled him.

Bo moaned when she pressed his ankle.

She straightened up and bumped her head against the lantern Quamana held. She rubbed at her forehead where the rim had caught her, but she didn't mention it. "I can't make it good as new," she said gazing at Bo's foot, "but I think I can straighten it out and maybe it'll heal." She took a deep breath. "Let's try it. Set the lantern down and crawl up on the bed. I want you to straddle Bo, facing me, and put all your weight into holding his leg steady."

Quamana hoped the cot would hold the weight of two men, and settled himself over Bo's hips. He wrapped his hands around the leg just below the knee.

"Ready?" she said.

He nodded. She got a grip on Bo's ankle, pulled it with slow gentle pressure, then more pressure, and then gave it a very slight turn. Quamana felt the bone behind the calf move in his hands.

She probed the foot with her fingers, gauging the position of the bones. "Not good," she said. "The ankle either. He'll be lame, but I don't think he'll lose his foot. You can get off now."

She wrapped the foot and the ankle in yards of white linen. "Could have been worse, you know. Could have had a compound fracture with the bone sticking out into the open air."

Quamana didn't answer her. She didn't seem to expect him to. She was nothing like any other white woman he'd seen. In fact, he'd never seen one up close like this. Had never been spoken to by a white woman, now that he thought about it.

"Don't let him put this foot on the floor. Not for weeks. No weight on it at all. Crawley won't like that, but I'll talk to Mr. Brown. Bo is to stay in this bed, or he can sit on the stoop if you carry him there. In a week or so, he can probably use a crutch as long as he keeps the wrappings tight."

"All right," Quamana nodded. He could move into Bo's cabin for a while, until Pierre could get him a crutch made.

"Now," she said, her hands on her hips. "Let's have a look at your arm."

Quamana took a step back. "I'll take care of it."

She advanced on him anyway until he was backed against the rough-hewn table. She untied the bloody cloth and prodded the skin around the gash. "Bled plenty. That's good. I'll just sew it up, good as new. Except you'll have a nasty scar." She glanced at his face. "But you know all about scars."

She got what she needed from her bag. "Sit down," she said and gestured to the one chair in the cabin. She slathered ointment into the gash with her fingers. With black silk thread, she sewed the edges together.

"I know it hurts," she said softly though Quamana had not moved, nor gasped, nor even winced.

Her head was bent over his arm. With the merest turn of his face, Quamana would be able to feel a wisp of her hair against his skin. But she was not just a woman. She was a healer. He respected that. And she was white.

She looked up then, as if he'd spoken. Quamana held his breath. Her hands stilled as she took in the ritual scars on his face, then lingered on his lips. When she met his gaze, he felt her awareness. She was a woman. He was a man. No more than that, but Quamana was strangely moved by this small recognition.

Then she tied off her stitches and wrapped his arm in white linen. After she packed her bag, she felt Bo's forehead for fever and measured the pulse in his throat.

"He'll do," she said. With a business-like nod to Quamana, she left the cabin.

Quamana sat with Bo the rest of the afternoon. He was glad to have seen the marvel of the woman's red hair. He was glad to have met a white who could look at a slave and see a person.

Chapter Eight

Charles stuck his head into Cooksy's domain, drawn by the smell of sweet buns fresh out of the oven.

"Mister Charles," Cooksy said, a big smile on her broad face. "Get on in here, I give you a treat."

"Cooksy, you're a treat," he said, gallant as always with the only woman on the place not a little afraid of him. She held her cheek up and he gave her a kiss. "You put raisins in those buns?"

"I did. And a little orange peel." She swept the cat off a chair. "Sit down, I give you a cup of coffee."

Charles tossed his hat on a peg near the door and sat at the long plank table cluttered with pans and spoons, a bowl of lemons, and a blue jug of cream. It was always warm in here where Cooksy kept a fire going in the cold months, always aromatic, always welcoming. He and Cooksy had both been on the Deslondes place before Andry took them on. The Deslondes' place was not so large as Andry's and she'd slipped treats to every child on the plantation, a handful of raisins, a slice of orange, a sliver of cake meant for the master's table.

Lydia, the new girl, flitted to the coffeepot hanging near the fire and poured him a cup. Cooksy set a napkin and a plate with a handsome sugar-topped bun before him then sat down to pass the time while Lydia darted from hearth to table to dry sink to water keg. Like a hummingbird, Charles thought.

"The new girl working out?" he asked Cooksy. The cat jumped into his lap and he ran a hand over its ears and down its back.

"Lydia? She's a fine girl," she said, pouring cream in his coffee. "Not much meat on her bones, but we'll get her plumped up. Trouble is she never still, not a minute, so she burn up all my good cooking. Lydia," she called, "come over here."

"Yes'm?" Lydia flitted over and stood with her little hands loosely clasped in front of her. She was a tiny thing, a little plain, but with a smile that lit her whole face.

Charles wiped the sugar off his mouth. "You settling in all right?" he asked.

"Yessir, Mr. Charles." She looked at Cooksy and smiled again. "This a good place."

Charles looked at Cooksy's kind face. "Yes, it is."

Cooksy patted Charles's hand and heaved herself to her feet. "You drink your coffee. I got biscuits to get in the oven."

Charles remembered that day when he saw Lydia again a week later. He was striding past the cook house when she came into the yard to toss a bucket of dish water into the parsley patch. She moved like an old woman, slow and stooped. The little hummingbird had become a crone. He was so struck by the change that he broke his stride.

"Lydia?"

She looked up, and then he understood. A dark scab an inch long marked her cheek. Gilbert had been at her. He'd had her and he'd cut her.

"Yessir?" Lydia's eyes were dull, her voice quiet.

His whole body burned, but he willed his hands to stay loose, his face to stay calm. What could he say to her? He hadn't protected her. He couldn't protect her.

Cooksy stepped into the yard and at sight of her loving face, he suddenly wanted to weep. He swallowed and caught her eye.

"You'll take care of her?"

"Course I will, Charles," she said. "Course I will. She gone be all right by and by."

He nodded stiffly and walked on, his own shoulders squared. A few more weeks, the rains would come. *You'll have your justice,* he imagined whispering in Lydia's ear. *Soon.*

The same afternoon, Charles and the carpenter crew laid out the dimensions for the new saw mill with pegs and string. Andry had handed him a blue print he'd gotten from his factor in New Orleans, so Charles didn't have to imagine the whole thing from top to bottom, for which he was grateful. He'd never built anything more complicated than the rendering shed for boiling down the sugar, and large as it was, it was just a shed.

Charles straightened up from bending over the peg he'd just tied. He'd spent too many hours in the saddle and not enough time doing hard labor like these men. His back ached. And then Gilbert Andry strolled up to watch the laying out.

He wore his polished high-top boots. "Modeled after those worn by Napoleon himself," Gilbert had boasted the day they arrived from his boot maker in New Orleans. His bright blue pantaloons and darker blue velvet jacket contrasted with the whiteness of his linen and lace. A very fine get-up for a man walking about among his cattle.

Charles could not bear to look at him. The man was scum, a rapist, a tormentor, a depraved soul. From the corner of his eye, he could see Gilbert tapping his riding crop against the side of his boot. Was it part of his look, or protection? A riding crop would not save him once it began.

Charles waited him out so that Gilbert was the first to speak. Small satisfaction, but Charles savored it.

"So, Charles, you're laying out the shape for the sawmill, I see."

Charles nodded, his eyes on the men stretching string between the pegs.

Gilbert's riding crop tapped a few more times against his boot.

"Good work crew you have here."

Charles had not forgotten the defeated sag to Lydia's shoulders, nor the hopeless hurt in her eyes. She might have been a virgin, little Lydia. She certainly had not been hardened enough by life to shrug off an assault. Gilbert had probably hurt her. He'd like that, hurting her, even before he took his knife to her cheek.

"I said, good work crew you have here," Gilbert repeated.

Charles turned to him, willing himself into a column of ice. Ice didn't kill fast and hot like flame did. And Charles could not kill Gilbert Andry, not today. He forced himself to nod.

He could see Gilbert's insecurities rising to the surface. His father's minion only nodded to him? His father's slave did not answer respectfully with a "Yes, sir, Mr. Gilbert. A fine crew"?

Charles used to wonder why the master's son sought him out around the plantation. If he had a new horse, a new saddle, anything he could boast about, Gilbert found a moment to sidle up to him. Charles used to think maybe Gilbert expected him to be envious of the fine things he showed off. Then he realized it was Charles's approval pretty little Gilbert wanted. The irony amused him, and revealed to him the privileged blond boy, heir to wealth and power, did not have it in him to become a man.

Charles let the silence grow between them, his gaze on his crew. Gilbert's crop began the tap tap tap against his leg again.

He snickered, like a horse. Charles glanced at him.

"You had the new little gal in the cook house yet?" Gilbert said.

Charles turned face-on to Gilbert then.

Maybe Gilbert sensed the tension in Charles' shoulders, but he didn't heed the danger Charles felt must be coming off him in waves. Instead of remaining silent, or changing the subject, or removing himself from the site, Gilbert tittered.

"She's a tiny little thing, real real tight, if you know what I mean. When it's their first time, it's real good. Usually, you know, for a man like me with an extra-large cock, a woman who's been used is fine, you know what I mean? But this one, she was sweet and easy. You'll like her, you haven't tried her yet."

Charles didn't allow his mouth to sneer, his jaws to tighten, nor his brows to rise. All he did was stare at this creature.

Gilbert tapped the riding crop faster and chuckled. If the man got any more nervous, he would giggle next. Charles hated that giggle.

Gilbert pointed a finger at him. "You must have had every woman on the place by now."

It would be easy to reach out and grab that finger and bend it back, forcing Gilbert to his knees. He wouldn't quit bending it back once the dirt soiled the fine pantaloons, either. He'd keep bending it until it snapped. There wouldn't be any more chuckles after that.

"I bet half these little niggers running around the place come from the loins of Charles Deslondes, eh? I'll soon catch up to you though, you wait and see." And then Gilbert giggled.

If Charles touched him, he would kill him. And then Andry would kill Charles. And what would happen to the rebellion then?

Gilbert wasn't worth it. Charles walked away and took up a handful of pegs.

Chapter Nine

Charles rode through the dawn, a light fog off the river cold on his face. He was stealing an hour to see Annique, leaving the first of the day's chores in George's capable hands.

Something had changed in him since she'd asked him to be hers. He smiled more. He even laughed. The calico he'd brought her had amused them all one long cold evening. They began by trying to recreate the intricate headdresses he'd seen the negresses wear in New Orleans, but Annique had never seen anything but simple head rags, and he was hopeless at trying to recreate the intricate folds. Instead, he experimented with the length of cloth, using it to decorate other parts of her body. He grinned even now, remembering how they'd played, and loved.

She learned on her own how to tie her calico into pretty folds and tuck the ends in securely. He wished he could give her pearls and rubies, but she swore she didn't want them. When they jumped the broom, she declared, she'd feel all dressed up and pretty in her blue and red and purple tignon.

He'd never thought to join himself with a woman that way. Who would have him, him with his secrets and his grim face? He knew what they called him behind his back. The Reaper. The slaves didn't fear him overmuch, he didn't think they hated him, but who could cross the distance he put between him and them? How could he let anyone get close to him when the next day might see him uncoil his whip to enforce the discipline a plantation demanded. Only Annique had ever come in, past the circle of cold he kept around himself. He felt a surge of gratitude for the warmth she brought with her, a wash of humility that he needed her and had not even known it.

They could have children together. A fine thing, to have a son. He'd never dreamed of it, until now. And a baby girl who smiled like her mother. He'd seen little ones wrap their tiny hands around their daddy's finger, seen them plant sloppy open-mouthed kisses on their cheeks. His throat tightened at the enormity of it.

Children of his own. A woman, Annique, his own. His heart was not so hard as he'd believed.

But what made her think of jumping the broom with him? Where did she ever get an idea he was the kind of man to tie yourself to? He was confused by it. What did she see in him? What did she expect of him? She would be content with his coming over a couple of times a week, year after year? Or maybe she thought eventually one master or the other would let them be together, living in the same cabin, sleeping in the same bed every night. But none of that would matter. Soon she could sleep where she pleased. If he were lucky, he'd still be alive for it to be in his bed.

A great blue heron flew over his head, looking for the perfect bayou to stalk frogs and little fish. A fine, clear morning. The frost on the grass would be gone in an hour, but for now, the world had a silvery coat to complement the pale gray sky above. Charles liked winter. He liked the way sound carried in cold air, his horse's hoofs striking the ground with a sharp clear tone. Winter nights were long, but he could sit by his fire and if he were careful, he could read from the two books he had hidden away, could think and plan. He could be himself, alone, unseen, unheard. But it was lonely, too, those long nights. What if Annique sat across the rough little table in the evenings, working her needle or nursing a babe? A life worth fighting for.

Quamana had come to him, had made his way in the dark through the fields between James Brown's place and Andry's. The man was like a giant cat, so silent and stealthy not even the dogs had picked up on his presence.

"When?" Quamana had demanded.

They plagued him with this question. Didn't they know the day they revolted would be Armageddon? Judgment Day? The end of the world as it had been? Many of them would die. If they failed, all of them would die.

Quamana had sat at his table, in the dark, his deep voice low and urgent. "Our people are getting restless. Their patience is worn down. Carnival is coming. The whites are thinking about their pleasures. We're ready. What are you waiting for, Charles?"

What could he tell him? That Annique had asked him to jump the broom? That he wanted, craved, that little bit of happiness, of normalcy, of life as other men knew it before he died?

Charles wiped a hand over his mouth. "It will be bloody, Quamana."

"Yes. We know this."

Sitting there, his friend's body merely a darker shade of black in the night, Charles realized he was afraid. He had not known that about himself, that he feared the awful carnage to come, the blades slicing into flesh, the screams.

Fear. He was grateful for the darkness so Quamana could not see it in his face. But maybe it was on him like a scent his friend could detect across the table.

"You read to us from your book," Quamana said. "You told us a man has a right to be free, to own his own labor, his own body. You have said this is worth dying for."

Charles drew a deep breath. "Yes."

"And do you believe it still?"

"Yes, Quamana. I believe it still. But we do this for all of us, not just for ourselves. If we rush into this headlong, we will surely lose ourselves and our chance. There will not be another in our generation, for our warriors will be vanquished, our bodies left to rot in the open for the birds and the ants."

"Charles, there are many of us between here and New Orleans. Few know your name, know who you are. But they depend on you. They believe in you. They await you. And know this. These men are not like the cows in the field. They are race horses, every one, prancing at the starting line, eager. Ready. We cannot let this readiness slip away."

"Yes," Charles said. "I understand." Quamana was right. The men were chafing at the wait. He had known for months the best time would be mid-January when his diary showed a high likelihood of rain, heavy rain. That was not so very long now, maybe five more weeks, but he couldn't risk telling anyone. Not even Quamana. Not yet.

"And so it will be soon," Quamana stated.

"Yes," Charles had said. "Soon."

But this morning, on his way to Annique, Charles pushed all that away. This morning, he would live and he would love and he would hope and dream.

A thin trail of smoke rose from Annique's chimney, and a few slaves were moving about down in the quarters, but the morning was yet silent and still. Charles kneed his horse toward the hitching post when the plank door opened in Annique's cabin.

François Trépagnier stepped onto the porch and paused, his attention on his flint as he lit the end of his cigar and drew on it.

Behind him, Annique stood in the doorway, a shawl thrown over her nightdress.

Charles, a man once made of blood, heart, and soul became a man of cold hard stone. Annique, her beautiful black hair around her shoulders, tousled, mauled by the man who called himself her master – her eyes found his. Once he might have drowned in the ocean of hurt he saw in her eyes. He might have wanted to save her and comfort her. But Charles, who had never known any warmth but hers, lost in that instant the part of himself that could love and care.

Trépagnier saw him now, a small smile pulling at his mouth. Wordlessly, he stepped off the porch and sauntered toward the big house for his breakfast.

Annique's body jerked into motion. She strode across the porch, down the steps, her hand stretched out to him. "Charles," she pleaded.

She was coming for him. He couldn't let her touch him. He didn't know what would happen to him if she touched him. Perhaps he would shatter like a hot stone plunged into cold water. Perhaps he would wail, his cry frightening the birds from the trees, and never be able to cease wailing. He only knew he would be broken if she reached him.

He dug his heels into his mount and pulled him back, turning him. Annique was close now, reaching for him. "Charles. Don't leave me! Charles!"

He spurred the horse and left her in the lane, calling after him.

He rode, pushing his horse for speed, for distance. His mind jumbled the images of his mother, the red-faced master laboring over her while he crouched in the corner, and Annique, his Annique, lying under the naked white man, her body fouled by his penetration, by his seed. His throat burned as if he'd swallowed lye, red hot iron bands squeezed his chest, yet he spurred the horse on, racing him down the river road, away, away.

That early morning, before her world shattered, Annique had wakened with a smile on her face. Those moments before the sun rose were her own. No pots to set boiling, no stirring stick to pull through the tubs of dirty clothes, nobody telling her to do this, do that. She snuggled deeper into her quilt and dreamed, planned, hoped.

The day Charles jumped the broom with her, Annique meant to creep into the master's garden and snip a camellia blossom off his prize bush. She would sneak it back to the quarters in her apron and then she'd poke the stem into her fancy tignon and be as prettified as a queen. All her friends would stand in a circle around them, and she and Charles would hop over the broom while everybody clapped and sang. Then they'd all drink a little white lightning in their spring water and eat sweet cakes to celebrate.

It was going to be a fine day when Charles stood up with her. She knew he was a difficult man, a man who held himself close. But he was loosening up a little. When he let himself laugh, when he let her tease him and his eyes lit up like there was peace and joy inside him, her Charles was a fine sight, and he loved her. She knew that. He'd never say it, but when he touched her like she was precious, she knew. And when he thrust himself inside her until his whole body shook with need, she knew. Charles was her man. And she was his woman.

He'd give her a baby first thing, if he hadn't already. She was late. She might already be carrying a little Charles Deslondes inside her. And that was another fine thing.

She heard a footstep on her porch and her pulse quickened. Charles had come to her. She sat up in bed, a smile on her face.

The door opened to lantern light, and holding the lantern was the master, his linen shirt open at the neck, his ugly white face eager. His member, already big and hard, strained against his pantaloons.

"Good morning."

Annique's smiled died on her face. Quickly she held her features still, as blank a face as she could conjure. But in her chest, her heart pounded and in her ears, the sound of blood rushing through her veins drowned out everything but the master's voice.

Trépagnier set his lantern on her table and started opening the buttons of his britches. "When I'm here, you are to call me François. I want to hear you say my name. And when I come," he said as he shucked his pants off his hips, "I want you to shout it out."

"Yes, sir."

He sat on her chair, took off his boots and pulled his pants over his ankles and feet. When he rose, he pulled his member free of his shirttail and revealed himself, erect and ready. He touched himself as he approached the bed.

"Let me hear you say it, girl."

"Yes, sir."

"Say my name."

"François."

"Good girl." He pulled the covers off her. "Take that gown off you."

Annique stared at him. His eyes seemed deep and black in his face, his form backlit by the lantern. Her throat seemed to close off her breath. She didn't want him to touch her. She didn't want him or his thing in her bed, in her body.

"Girl," he said. In some corner of her mind, Annique registered that there was no menace in his voice. The master didn't need menace to tell a slave woman to spread her legs. He knew she would.

What if she didn't? Annique allowed herself to imagine such a thing. Tell him "No, master." Tell him she didn't want him, to put his pants on and leave her cabin. She imagined he'd laugh. And if she resisted him? If she kicked or scratched? He'd beat her. He might even punch her in the belly where maybe she had Charles's baby growing.

Annique pulled her nightdress over her head but kept it in front of her chest, shielding her from his gaze. Her own focus was the far wall, gray but yellowed now by the lantern light.

Master took the gown from her and tossed it on the floor. "Lay back."

He climbed into the bed beside her. "You got the sheets nice and warm, girl."

Annique hardly knew what he did to her. She went away, her eyes open but her gaze on a world where butterflies played among the wildflowers and a sweet-water stream burbled through a meadow.

When his time came and his body tightened, he told her again, "Say my name."

She remembered then where she was. "François," she whispered.

"Louder," he grunted.

71

"François!" she shouted, and he spurted hot seed into her body.

No matter, she told herself. She would wash it out, soon as the master left, she would fill a wash tub with water hot as she could stand, pour a jug of vinegar in it, and lower herself into the tub, let the hot sour water wash the master's white spurt out of her. There'd be no white baby in her belly. Not ever. She knew what the old women said. She knew what to do.

The master rolled off her, lay back on the narrow cot, squeezing her against the wall, and put his hands behind his head. "You got a good ass on you, girl. Charles like that ass, eh?"

He didn't seem to expect an answer. She gave none.

Soon his body cooled in the early morning chill. He got up, dressed himself, then patted a pocket looking for his cigar.

Annique pulled the nightdress over her head and wrapped her shawl around her. He would leave now. She would put her worn shoes on, the ones he gave her and all the other slaves last Christmas, and she would run to the washhouse and start the water to boiling. Auntie would help her, maybe add some of her herbs to the water to help purify her insides.

Annique's head came up suddenly. A horse's hooves, a jangle of harness? God, no. No.

The master stepped onto the porch to light his cigar, no need of the lantern now the sun was peeping through the trees. Annique grasped the door jamb, hardly able to stand. And there he was, Charles.

There was nothing in his face. Nothing. His mouth was still, his brows, still. But his eyes. He glanced at the master, but his eyes were all for her. And there, in their dark depths, there was nothing.

He wouldn't even give her his anger, his hurt? Even his disgust, even his hatred would be better than this.

"Charles," she said. She found her strength and let go of the door jamb. She strode into the yard, her arm stretched out to him. If only she could touch him. She would make him understand. She would make him forgive her.

But he backed his horse from her, he turned its head.

"Charles, don't leave me!"

He did, though. Charles left her on her knees in the dirt, her arms stretched out for him.

Late that afternoon, Charles sent his people home for the day. They'd put in an easy nine hours, but there was a chill in the air, seeping into a body's bones. And they had chores of their own to do before it got dark.

He followed them in from the field, trailing behind Caleb and Baby Ann walking together. Caleb carried her hoe and his over his shoulder. She leaned in to him as they walked down the lane. Now and then he'd dip his head to catch what she said. Charles looked away, but his eyes strayed back to the pair of them, always a touch of elbows or shoulder or hand.

He only thought he'd turned to stone. Pain seared through him, burning the flesh of his heart. Lovers. Caleb still loved Baby Ann. Master Andry had taken his woman, yet Caleb put his arm around her waist and pulled her close as they strolled toward the little cabin they called their own.

Charles turned away, undone by a love he couldn't understand. What of the humiliation? The rage? The betrayal? How could Caleb look at Baby Ann and not see her naked body pressed into the mattress, the master's white ass humped over her? Did Caleb not bleed inside every time he looked at her?

Charles turned on his heel and strode back toward the fields, darkening now as the shadows from the border trees lengthened across the turned-over earth. How could Annique have let the master in her door, much less her bed? She couldn't have fended him off? Sweet-talked him into leaving her alone? Hadn't she said she wanted to be his, only his? Why hadn't she fought? The only thing in this world he had ever wanted for himself, the only person he had ever allowed himself to love, and she had betrayed him. He could not forgive her.

He squeezed his eyes shut, his trudging through the plowed earth aimless.

He knew he was unjust. There was not a woman on the river who could say no to her master. He knew that. But his heart burned with shame and anger and god-awful hurt.

He should never have allowed himself to love her. His life was meant for other things – for justice, for retribution. What a fool he'd been to let himself live for her. He admitted it to himself now. Quamana was right – ''he had been delaying. He'd been too greedy for a little more of living, of love, of Annique to commit himself to a date. Because deep in his soul, he did not expect to survive the rebellion. There was a chance they would succeed, a chance they would prevail and all these slaves along the river would be free, their labor their own, their bodies, their women, their children. But he could not see himself among them.

He would look again at the Almanac, at the coming phases of the moon, the likeliest days for rain in the next month. He would set the day.

Chapter Ten

Living somewhere behind his eyes had become Quamana's normal existence. His body registered cold, heat, tired muscles and aching bones from hard labor and not enough rest. His mind, though, paid no heed to the physical world. He was not like Kook, who somehow had made a life for himself in spite of his bondage. Kook allowed himself a woman, and children. He even allowed himself to love them.

Not Quamana. Memory ruled his nights. The woman he'd left in the village when he went to war, how proud he'd been when he'd taken the bride price to her father. They'd lain together, her flesh yielding and sweet, her sighs quiet in the night. His son had been at her breast when he left her.

She would tell the boy his father had been a great warrior. She would tell him his father was dead.

He no longer went to the widow women in the slave quarters who welcomed him to their beds. He no longer sat with the other slaves in the evening to talk or sing or tell stories. He was one thing only. A flame, hot and steady, ready to set off a conflagration that would burn the marks of slavery from every soul on the river.

Sometimes the flame inside him grew so hot he thought his body would ignite. A curtain of red would color his vision and his hands would fist of their own accord. To slash, to burn, to kill the white man––his destiny sucked at him.

But he waited. He waited, and he watched. It would be soon.

Early morning, Quamana felt he had only just fallen asleep when the overseer's first bell woke him. The air was cold, the breath of the two other bachelors in his cabin visible in the weak light.

Young Remo, still pained by his limbs and his backbone growing in the night, slept on. Alphonse, the hollow-chested, weak-chinned man no woman would keep in her bed, rolled out of his cot. It seemed to bring him pleasure waking Remo in the mornings. He stepped over to the young one, bent to his ear and shouted, "Get up, boy!" Remo, as always, jerked awake, his eyes startled, his body tensed. Alphonse chuckled and thumped him on the forehead with his knuckle.

Reason enough to kill the man, Quamana thought. But Alphonse was Remo's problem.

The slaves emerged into the chilly morning, the mist still coming off the ground as the sun's weak light turned the sky pearl gray. Ahead of him, Kook and Rosie delivered their children to Serafina, the old woman who kept the little ones during the day. Rosie stooped to wipe the breakfast gruel off her son's mouth and give him a kiss. Kook stepped onto the porch and handed his baby Lila to Serafina.

"Gone need more firewood, a cold day like this," she said.

"Yes, ma'am. I'll get it."

Quamana fell into step with Kook on the way to the woodpile. They each gathered an armload and carried it back to Serafina's. They made a neat stack on the porch and then followed the others to the bell yard to see where the overseer wanted them that day. That drainage ditch full of snakes still needing cleaning out. Quamana tried not to smile since Kook walked right next to him, but there was nothing more fun than watching Kook pretend he wasn't afraid of snakes.

But something was wrong. Ahead, the people stood like statues, arms at their sides, not a murmur, not a motion in the whole crowd. Beyond them huddled a coffle of slaves chained one behind another. The slavers were here.

The master himself waited, his arms crossed over his big belly, his feet spread apart. Beside him stood a tall greasy-headed man with a whip coiled at his belt who eyed them as they gathered.

So Master Brown needed funds and meant to sell off some of his stock to, what, pay a gambling debt? Buy a new racehorse? Present his missus with a strand of pearls for Christmas?

Crawley separated the men from the women and stepped back for Brown and the slaver to look them over. Quamana felt the knife sheathed at the small of his back. If he were chosen—he wouldn't go. He and the others, they were too close now to give it all up. The slavers would have to kill him before he'd be shackled again, but he'd take some of them with him into hell before he died.

He stood with Kook among the other slaves. He looked them over, these men he labored with, lived with. They're like sheep, he told himself. Docile, stupid. Stunned, helpless, and scared.

Quamana was furious with them, with himself. With Charles Deslondes for the delay. They should have acted before now. They should have risen last week, or the week before. Before this...atrocity. Or maybe this is what they needed to remind them what they were. Cattle. No more than livestock to be traded and prodded and hobbled.

Quamana had a hard time understanding such men. Why did they live like oxen, or mules, and never protest? Did they believe what the priest told them, that it was God's will they should labor like beasts in this world, to be rewarded only in the next? Or maybe they knew only slavery and could not imagine freedom, like deaf men who had never heard a bird sing or a woman sigh, and had no understanding of what they missed. And there were those, he knew, who allowed their lives to be ruled by fear.

Too many of these men were weak souls, defeated and hopeless. But others, like him, would only be more hardened that Brown could so casually rend a husband from his wife, a mother from her child. Kook, though his expression was ever mild and pleasant, had fire in his belly. He too had a knife hidden under his shirt. And there stood Billy John, his jaw knotted, his body tense.

He looked for Rosie standing with the women. She was a worthy woman who had her own fires to keep banked. Now though he saw fear in her eyes as she gazed at Kook in silent plea.

Brown strolled along the line of men, the slaver at his elbow, Crawley trailing behind. They paused now and then for the slaver to poke at this one or that one. Open your mouth, he said to Remo. But Remo had bad teeth, young as he was, three or four of them already gone.

They walked right past Alphonse, his slight frame and weasely face not likely to bring either of them a profit. When they came to Louis, the slaver stopped.

"Let's have a look at this one. Step out here, boy."

Louis, a man of middling height but in his prime, left the line, his legs stiff, his eyes blank. The slaver grabbed his biceps, gave it a squeeze. Ran his hand over his rump, down to thigh and calf, feeling the muscle.

"Take your shirt off," he said.

Louis's eyes found his woman across the yard.

Crawley jabbed him with the butt of his whip. "You heard him. Take it off."

Louis dropped his jacket to the ground and pulled the shirt over his head.

"No whip marks on this one," Crawley offered. "Never any trouble. Good worker."

"Open your mouth," the slaver said.

Quamana eyed the men and women chained in the coffle. They stood with their shoulders slumped, barefoot in the cold, their faces closed to all feeling. They'd already endured the separation from their wives, husbands, old mothers, children. Now they were mute and numb. He dismissed them. They were of no use even to themselves.

Louis stood there with his mouth open wide as the slaver stuck a grimy finger in and shoved against his teeth. Quamana despised Louis for being a "good" slave. He and Kook already knew him as one of those who'd made his peace with being the white man's chattel. They did not count Louis as one of them.

What if they started the rebellion, right here, right now? Just him and Kook, and maybe Billy John. The others would join them once they saw that white men bleed as easily as black.

Quamana closed his eyes. Crawley wore a pistol in his belt; the master had another in his holster. Two slavers stood nearby with rifles on their hips, another on a mule with a shotgun. But they were only six, these armed white men. If they acted together, men and women and boys, they could kill them all. The rifles would go off, the shotgun, the pistol—some of them would die——but they would be slaves no more.

Quamana opened his eyes. It wasn't going to happen. Not today. These others, they were not warriors. Louis would accept his fate. The knife nestled in the hollow of Quamana's back would stay in its sheath. For now.

"I'll give you $500 for this one," the slaver said.

Brown shook his head. "Ridiculous. This one is prime stock. Look at that chest, that belly. All muscle, this one. $900, and you got yourself a deal."

"He a breeder?"

Brown looked to Crawley for the answer.

"Yeah, had a cabin full of younguns till the cholera couple years back. Got one left, I reckon."

The slaver's eyes slid to the boy just behind Louis. He was maybe twelve, a good size on him for being too young for his growth spurt. "This one his?"

"Yeah, that's the one."

The slaver turned the boy around, looked at his hands, already calloused from wielding a hoe.

"His feet are big," Crawley said. "Means he'll be a tall one."

"You a good boy?" the slaver asked.

The boy's eyes darted to his father. Quamana saw the trembling in his limbs, knew he was close to panic. His father touched the boy's hand, steadying him.

"No trouble out of either one of them," Crawley said.

James Brown, master of this land, this water, this soil. Owner of these women, men, and children, of the dirt under their fingernails, the teeth in their heads, the skin on their backs, the bones under their flesh. He looked at Louis, narrowed his eyes, looked at the boy, pursed his lips, measuring their worth.

"I can let you have both of them for $1500."

The slaver spit into the dirt. "Now, you know they ain't worth half that."

The master and the slaver walked off, haggling. Crawley motioned to Louis and the boy. A woman's wail tore the air, a cry as ragged as a rough knife tearing into her heart. Quamana felt the hair rise on the back of his neck.

The boy ran for his mother, but Crawley caught him and dragged him back. Quamana turned away. He knew this woman, Jamaica. He heard her laughing sometimes in the cabin next to his, heard her calling the boy in to supper in the evenings. He didn't want to see anymore, but he couldn't shut out Jamaica's shriek or her boy's cries.

The women took Jamaica's arms, held her up, held her back. Crawley raised his voice. "Go on to the back field, all of you. I be there in a quarter hour, and I'm gonna count heads, you better believe it."

The slaver's men shoved Louis into the line and shackled him, then the boy. They'd be taken to the market in New Orleans, and from there? No one here would ever know.

The women ran to their men, the need to touch and to hold greater than their fear of Crawley. Rosie grabbed Kook and hid her face against his chest. He wrapped his arms around her shuddering shoulders. "You'll be safe, I promise," he told her. "This will never happen to us. You know that."

Quamana frowned. That was loose talk. No slave can promise anything, not unless he means to be a slave no longer. He looked around to see who might have heard.

Alphonse stood just behind Rosie, his eyes on the ground. Quamana had seen Alphonse sidle up to the overseer and then, later that day or the next, someone would be put on short rations, or bound in the stocks, or even whipped. And the weasel had heard what Kook said.

Quamana followed him to the fields, watching.

All that day, the people hardly spoke. Some of the women cried as they hoed, keenly aware it could have been their children, their husbands who were taken away, not even given time to hug, to kiss before the slavers chained them and marched them down the river road.

Quamana worked close to Alphonse. When they broke for the mid-day meal, he watched the weasel takes his rations and sit a few feet away from Kook and Rosie. Quamana lowered himself to the ground a few feet behind him.

Kook and Rosie said very little. If Alphonse expected confirmation there was rebellion in the air, he was disappointed. What he'd heard that morning was enough, however, if he whispered it in Crawley's ear.

Before dusk, Crawley sent everyone back to the quarters. There was supper to cook, chores to get done before bedtime. Quamana, watching, always watching, saw his friends pick up their children from Serafina, saw Rosie hug Joshua to her, her shoulders shaking with sobs. Kook touched her hair and led her and the children to their cabin.

Quamana went on to the woodpile and chopped a load of firewood for Serafina, stacked it on her porch, and went to his own cabin. It was his turn to put the corn meal mush over the fire, to stir the pot of beans he'd put on a bed of coals that morning. He dished it up to Remo and to Alphonse and himself. They ate in silence, Quamana's brooding long since having squelched Remo's youthful chatter. Even Alphonse kept his gossip and his boasting to himself tonight.

As the quarters settled down, Quamana sat on the porch stoop and watched the stars come out. The night was chill, but he didn't notice the cold or the hard boards. He closed his eyes and listened to the whir of bat wings as they swooped through the night. Even here, half a world away from home, the bats made the dark alive.

Through the oiled paper and the shutters on Jamaica's window next door, he could hear her crying. She'd sent the women home to their own families and grieved in solitude, her windows unlit. He couldn't help her. He had nothing to offer her, but he wished she were not alone.

Remo came onto the porch and stood, listening. "Nobody over there with her," he said.

Quamana tipped his head toward Jamaica's cabin. "Go on."

He saw Remo hesitate in front of her door, wipe his hands on his pants, and then knock. He opened the door and stepped in. "I sit with you a while, you want," he said. The door closed behind him.

Quamana stepped off the porch and headed down the lane to walk off his restlessness. Maybe then he'd be able to sleep. All around, he heard the life of the quarters through the thin walls. Rosie's baby was fretful, maybe cutting a new tooth. Henri and his wife were fighting again. From Billy John's cabin, the sounds of sex. More babies, he thought. More chattel for Mr. Brown.

He walked through the peach grove, bare branches visible in the star light. No moon. He liked dark nights. He felt invisible walking the place, no one to see him, no one to notice whether he was even alive. These were the only moments of peace, moments when he remembered he was a creature on the earth like the bats and the frogs and the birds and that this life would be over just as theirs would be, and other men, other bats and birds would come after them.

He circled back to his own cabin, thinking he could sleep now. The back door opened and Alphonse's skinny figure slipped out. Quamana hung back in the shadows and watched him cross through the peach trees.

Silent as a jungle cat, Quamana followed Alphonse to the overseer's cabin. He heard Alphonse's quiet knock, saw the light through the cracks around the window. Crawley was still up.

The door opened and yellow light spilled onto the porch for a moment. Crawley stepped out and closed the door and they were in darkness once again. Their voices were low murmurs. If Alphonse was telling the overseer what Kook said...

Quamana eased the knife out of its sheath at the back of his waist and crept closer, the night darker under the live oaks. His blood was cool, his heartbeat steady.

From the dark, he rushed Alphonse, wrapped one arm around his neck and plunged the knife under his ribs. Crawley, too stunned to react, gave Quamana time to shove Alphonse's body at him. The overseer cried out and pushed the bloody corpse off him. Quamana struck, whipping his blade across Crawley's throat. The overseer went down, gurgling, dying.

Fast as thought, Quamana put his blade in Alphonse's hand and then felt for the knife the overseer wore at his belt. It was there, still in its sheath. He yanked it free, the man still strangling on his own blood.

"Mr. Crawley?" A woman's voice from inside the cabin. "Eugene?"

Quamana plunged Crawley's blade into Alphonse's lifeless body, then leapt off the porch and fled silently, swiftly into the dark.

Behind him, he heard Mrs. Crawley screaming, screaming, screaming. Her screams filled the whole world, echoed through the night, wakened every soul. In the quarters, windows lit up with candle flame.

He slowed as he approached the back side of his own cabin. People were beginning to open their front doors and venture into the lane. He mustn't be seen coming from the direction of the overseer's place, not even by other slaves.

Jamaica opened her back door and saw him in the starlight. They stared at one another.

"That Mrs. Crawley screaming?" she said quietly.

He nodded.

"You done rape?"

"No. Not that."

"Come on in here then."

He followed her inside. Remo slept on a pallet on the floor, oblivious to the commotion outside. At his age, it would take a lightning bolt to wake him.

Jamaica lit a candle and held it up. She saw the blood on his clothes, on his hands and arms. She nodded. "Strip off them clothes. I got water in the bucket over there."

She stirred the embers in her fireplace and fed the bloody clothes to the flames. "On that shelf, Louis' old pants and shirt."

On top of the clothes, Louis' pipe, the one he had whittled on summer evenings. Quamana set it aside carefully. The pants were short for him, but they didn't have to fit, they only had to be free of Crawley's and Alphonse's blood.

"Who you kill?" Jamaica asked.

He looked at her in the firelight. She held his gaze.

"Crawley. And Alphonse."

She let out a breath. "Ain't nobody gone miss Alphonse, but there gone be trouble over Crawley."

"Had to be done," he said.

"All right," she said at last. She looked at Remo breathing softly, his head cushioned on his arm. "Leave the boy be. We tell him you come in here with me after he fell asleep."

She looked out her front window at people gathering in the lane, listening to the screams and wails. There were shouts, now, too, coming from the big house.

"Come on, now. You and me go out in the lane together."

As they emerged from her cabin, Quamana saw a few nudge each other, looking at them, probably thinking he hadn't wasted any time getting into Jamaica's bed, but the drama of shouts and lanterns up at the overseer's house claimed their attention.

"You go, Serafina," Billy John said. "You the oldest. Won't nobody up there be mad with you."

"Well." She thought a moment. "I guess I go up there and see what I see."

Kook moved through the mingling crowd to Quamana's side. "You know anything about this?" he murmured.

Quamana gave him a slight nod.

When Serafina came back, Brown came with her carrying a lantern. He stood on the porch of Serafina's cabin to speak to them.

"Old Serafina here," Brown said, "tells me the dead nigger's name is Alphonse. He stuck a blade in Mr. Crawley, but Crawley got him, yes he did. They are both lying dead on the Crawley porch, two knives, two dead bodies."

Brown wiped his hand over his mouth. "A terrible thing, one of you killing a white man. Terrible. There got to be a reason for it. Any of you know what that reason is, I want you to come tell me. Won't be any harm to you, you come tell me why this nigger knocked on a man's door and killed him." He shook his head. "Terrible thing."

Brown looked at all of them. None of them had anything to say.

Brown picked up the lantern. "You know anything, you come see me," he said again and walked off the porch, through the gathered slaves, and back toward the bloody scene.

The slaves talked among themselves and began to drift back to their beds. Kook touched Quamana's arm and tilted his head toward his cabin. After a moment's hesitation, Jamaica followed.

Chapter Eleven

Sunday morning, Charles followed the people down the back lane to the little church the planters had put up for them behind Trouard's place. The masters paid a priest, too, to say the mass, to spend a few minutes each service reminding them they were God's children and they lived the life He meant for them to live. Charles had often wondered if the plantation owners told the priest to tell them that, or maybe it really was in the holy book that the black man was born to be the white man's slave. He didn't know. He didn't care.

He lagged behind, his belly full of acid and lead. Annique would be there. He didn't want to see her. It had been three days since Trépagnier stepped out of her cabin and shattered his heart. Three days of cold, bitter, hell. But his feet pulled him onward. He would not talk to her, not that, ever again. But to see her--he had to see her.

George and his family, Maisy and Old Gus, Caleb and Baby Ann disappeared into the whitewashed church, babes in arms, little ones by the hand. Charles couldn't go in. All the slaves from this stretch of the river would be close-packed in there, the air sickly sweet with incense. And Annique was in there.

He retreated to the orchard nearby and leaned against a pecan tree as the priest's high nasal tones filtered through the open door, calling them to prayer. He patted his pocket, looking for his pipe, then stuck it in his mouth and forgot to light it.

The priest would drone on at least an hour. He couldn't stand there, couldn't be still that long.

He moved down the rows, his eyes on the toes of his boots shuffling through the golden brown leaf litter, his mind at war with his heart. This confusion was new to him. Always, his mind had led him, his heart merely the repository of the rage his mind kept in check. But this pain. It was unbearable. It was beyond his understanding.

There was nothing unique in a black man knowing the white master took his woman, sometimes in the black man's own bed. Nothing new in the black man swallowing what pride he might have left after a lifetime of indignities. But it had never happened to Charles. He had never cared when he saw Andry's lantern bobbing through the night on the way to the quarters, never cared if the master bedded a woman Charles had himself bedded.

But those women had not been Annique. The image of Trépagnier stepping out her door, satisfied and smug, flashed across his brain over and over. When he couldn't stop himself, he even imagined the man's white hands on her dark skin, kneading her breasts, or in the darkest heart of the night, imagined the man's prick, red and ugly, pushing into her body. He had bit down on his fist to keep himself from pounding the walls in his torment. And when the sun rose again, he pulled on his boots, rang the bell, oversaw the crews, his face and body revealing nothing of his pain.

"Charles," she said.

His breath caught. She stood not ten feet away, a shawl wrapped around her shoulders. There were deep circles under her eyes and hollows in her cheeks. She looked drawn, like she hadn't slept, hadn't eaten. Well, neither had he.

"Charles," she said again.

His heart beat thudded in his ears, but his mind failed him. His body failed him. He couldn't think, couldn't move.

"Can't you forgive me?" she whispered.

His chest filled to bursting with something hot and viscous, the flood rising and choking him. Heat surged up behind his eyes, and tears, my God, scalding hot tears filled his eyes. If he didn't get away, he would reach for her. If he didn't get away from her he would drown.

His head shaking back and forth, he took a step back, and then another.

She stretched her hand to him. "Charles, please."

He turned on his heel and fled.

Annique dropped to her knees and then onto her hands, retching.

Chapter Twelve

Charles kept his eye on the slave he'd bought in New Orleans. Justice hadn't given him any trouble, but there was a tension in the man. If he had made friends with the others, if he had flirted with the women, slacked off his work when he could, Charles would have dismissed him as prime slave material, a man settling in to the new place fate had brought him to. But Justice held himself aloof. He ignored the women, and he worked himself hard from first light till the evening bell, burning off frustration and anger. Even more telling, whenever Justice lifted his eyes from the hoe, he scanned the horizon, betraying a yearning Charles knew very well.

Justice did not mean to stay. He meant to run. Charles could see it on him, but he could not let him do that, not now. He needed Andry and every other owner on the river comfortable and complacent, not stirred up by a runaway to wariness and increased vigilance. But Charles could use a man with the backbone, the stomach, the heart of a rebel.

Charles rode his horse between the neat rows his crew threw up the length of the field. Ahead of him, George hoed steadily, not slacking, not killing himself, just getting it done. George was near the same age he was, born and grown to manhood on this plantation. Had taken a wife. Had sired children. Went to church every Sunday and prayed to God. What did George pray for, Charles wondered? He showed no sign he ached for freedom as Justice did. He showed no sign of discontent with his lot in life.

Was it possible for an intelligent man to be as untroubled as George seemed? Was there no secret inner life contrary to his image as a contented slave?

Charles didn't know another slave who seemed to accept his bondage and yet carried himself with the self-respect and dignity that George did. He walked the earth as a man who knew who he was, who had no agenda, no secret life. *This* was his life, working like an ox in another man's fields, raising his sons so they didn't earn the lash or kill themselves running into the swamps. And every night, going home to a family, feeling love and joy even as he wore the white man's yoke. An alien creature, to Charles' mind.

And here he was, Charles, the white man's trusted favorite, his boots thick-soled, his canvas pants held up with a leather belt, his feet four feet off the ground. Fortunate, privileged, compared to George. But he had no woman, he had no sons.

Maybe if a man had not had a mother whispering in his ear every day of his childhood: *You a man, Charles. You let the white man think you his creature, you do what you have to do, but inside, you no man's slave.* Maybe George had a mother who told him, *Whatever your lot in life, you make the best of it. Even a slave can be a good man, George, a happy man. You live your life for what matters, the good air, and love, and taking care of your own. The rest, it be what meant to be, and you don't be gone change that.*

Maybe God, or more likely the Devil, Charles thought, laughed at him and all his fervor and ideals while George got on with living, his years spent on this patch of earth without torment, without rage and doubt and loneliness. Maybe Charles deserved the Devil's mockery.

He pulled his horse up and George leaned on his hoe. "Morning, Charles."

"Morning, George. Looks like you're near about finished with this field."

"Mid-day, we probably get it done."

"You been keeping an eye on the new man?"

"Justice? He a hard one, but he do his work."

"He settling in, making friends?"

George, the only slave on the place Charles felt he could have a conversation with, betrayed himself when his eyes shifted away. "He don't complain."

Charles's eye twitched. It shouldn't get to him, that even George distrusted him. He had known all his life that he could only be *other*. Not white, never that. But in spite of what his mother had drummed into him, he was not a black man either, not like George. His skin was lighter, his lot in life easier.

That otherness made him the man he was. Because he was other, because his mother had wheedled and stroked her master, his father, he had been taught to read. Because he was other, he could leave the plantation when he pleased. The master assumed he was visiting Annique, but he could also conspire with Mathurin, Kook, Quamana, and even Kenner and Chapin. Being other allowed him to lead this rebellion, to free not only himself, but every other black soul in Louisiana. Loneliness was a small price to pay for such a destiny.

"See can you help him settle himself. Can't have him running off."

George's eyes flicked to the whip looped on Charles's pommel. "I'll do that."

Charles nudged his horse on across the field. He had to see to the crew making rough planks out of that big cypress they'd felled. He could hear the chink of axes and the split of wood as wedges were hammered into the bole. When the sawmill was up and running, it would produce planks of pine, oak, and cypress, smooth and even, worth a fortune as this part of the territory grew. A fortune neither Andry nor Trépagnier would collect, but the men who earned it would.

If it wasn't harvest time, Andry gave his slaves Sundays off. They were expected to attend mass in the morning, and they needed, of course, to tend the animals, for horses, mules, oxen, pigs, chickens, sheep, and turkeys did not cease to be hungry on Sundays. The cooks had to cook for the master and his family, for they too were hungry even on Sundays. The maids served and the kitchen girls cleared away and washed the porcelain dishes carefully, dried them, and put them away along with all the silver and crystal. The house slaves made the beds, curled the ladies' hair, mended hems, polished shoes, emptied chamber pots, and answered sweetly when called on to do this little thing or that.

Other than that, the slaves had the rest of the day to work in their own gardens, mend their own worn clothing, see to their own firewood or leaky roof or split sole. Some found time to whittle or sew a toy, some won leave to visit a sweetheart on a nearby plantation. Some went into the near woods to hunt up a possum for the stew pot.

Charles himself had little to do on this Sunday before Christmas. He didn't have to tend the stock or mend his own clothes. It was too risky to bring out one of his books in daytime, so he didn't read. Andry knew he was literate, in fact depended on it now and then, but it would be ruinous to be found with these particular books.

He had acquired them on his first visit to New Orleans when he was still a stripling. Andry had brought him along to tend the horses and had given him the afternoon to entertain himself. Down on the broad levee, among dozens of other vendors, an old man had a book stall. His hair was nappy, but his skin showed he had white ancestors as well as black. A free man, Charles understood. He watched the man awhile, thinking about the fact that the man had no master, no one telling him what to do and when to do it, no man using up his days, his body, his being. He wondered if the old man had been born free, or made free.

Charles gave himself a mental shake. He was a slave, and his father had not chosen to free him, in spite of his mother's prodding. But he could read, and no man owned what was in his head.

Charles shifted his attention to the books. He stood to the side, trying to read the titles without being noticed. Of course he couldn't buy a book, even though he had money in his pocket from writing out blind old Mrs. Hendry's letters on the plantation north of Andry's. But in town among strangers, a slave better keep his illicit literacy to himself, so he only watched as other people, white people, picked through the books.

For a while, no one came to the stall and Charles inched closer, his neck craned to read the book spines. The old man spoke quietly. "Come here, boy," he said in the lilting French of the islands.

Charles approached him cautiously.

The old man spoke in hushed tones. "Somebody has taught you to read?"

Charles could have run off through the crowds. He could have widened his eyes and said, "No, sir. I cain't read. 'Course I cain't read." But he could, he could read! He took a chance. With the merest nod, he admitted it.

"You got money?"

Charles nodded again, his breath coming fast and shallow.

"How much you got in your pockets?" Charles had heard the same melodic speech among the slaves brought over from Haiti, their masters having escaped the great rebellion there.

Charles held out his hand, showing the man his coins.

The vendor raised his eye brows. "That's a lot of money for a slave. You steal that from your master?"

Charles closed his fist and gave the man a black look. "I am not a thief."

The bookseller searched Charles' face. "You like being a slave?" he murmured.

Charles snapped his head back as if he'd been slapped. Then he remembered. Slaves did not express dissatisfaction with their lot in life. Not to a white stranger, not to a black stranger, and not to a half-black stranger either. He veiled his thoughts behind an impassive face.

"Hhn," the man snorted. "Maybe you not as dumb as you look."

Young enough to be insulted, Charles started to edge away.

"Hold on, boy," the bookseller said, his face grim now. "Maybe you the one I been hoping for. Maybe you the one gone take up the cause." He crossed his arms and looked around as if surveying the crowd for customers. "I'm going to hand you two books," he said, his voice hardly above a whisper. "Don't let nobody, I mean nobody, catch you with these books. You understand?"

Charles had heard there were books about women and the things men could do with them. Some of them even had pictures. Is that what the old man had?

But there was nothing in the man's face to hint these books were about pleasures. Or even sin. Maybe the bookseller really had come from Haiti where all the slaves were made free. He'd heard the men, at night, in the quarters as the fire died down, talk about the revolution there, about the slaves who'd come over with their masters fleeing the chaos. Those refugees were still slaves. But some black Haitians, now free, had come to New Orleans. There were whispers that these men meant to bring the glorious revolution to Louisiana.

This bookseller might have been in the rebellion himself. He might be one of those who worked in the shadows to make what happened in Haiti happen here.

That thought lured Charles closer. "I understand," he whispered.

In a voice a little louder than necessary, the man said, "Yes, I have the books your master wanted."

The man bent down behind his stall and rummaged through a box for brown paper and string. From another box, covered over with a burlap cloth, he picked through the books and came up with two volumes, both badly worn and frayed on the edges. Keeping low so that passersby could not see the titles, he wrapped them in the paper and tied the string around them.

He stood up. Held his hand out for Charles's money. When the coins had crossed his palm, he hesitated. "You're a slave, boy, don't say you're not." He hardly moved his lips as he spoke. "These books are worth your life. You still want them?"

Worth his life? Charles's mind raced. If the man had been a revolutionary in the great revolt, then these books--

"Decide!" the man hissed as two gentlemen approached the stall.

"Yes!"

"Take those directly to your master," the man said loudly. "No loitering, now."

Charles clutched the books to his chest and rushed through the crowds back to the stable where he'd left the horses and carriage. Andry might let him read a book, maybe. But not if they were books about the revolution. Charles knew that much even if he were only half grown. He checked that the ostler was busy with a gentleman who wanted to hire a wagon.

He searched the carriage, behind the cushions, under the seats. No place to hide them inside the carriage. He ran his hands on the underside, in the luggage compartment. Then he heard Andry's booming voice as he came in and offered the ostler payment for the horses' oats. No time. He tossed the brown package into the tight space beneath the driver's seat. Andry could see the books plain as day from where he stood. Charles hopped up and took his place, his feet cradling the package between them. And then he prayed.

"All right, boy. Let's go home," Andry called to him and heaved himself into the carriage. The vehicle rocked and then settled. Charles chucked to the horses and they set off up the river, Charles feeling like a hot brick rested between his ankles.

Now the precious books lay hidden under the floorboards in Charles's cabin as he walked deep into the woods. He had no meeting with his confederates planned, but sometimes he just needed to be alone, away from all the eyes on the place, blue, brown, or black.

He carried a Girandoni rifle on his shoulder. Charles's father, Monsieur Jacques Deslondes, had passed on to him this relic from the Austrian army before he died, his one moment of familial acknowledgement. The gun was a large bore air rifle capable of bringing down a deer, maybe even a bear, with its .45 pellets.

Charles was in no hurry. He knew these woods well, several miles on either side of Andry's place and miles back from this stretch of the river where the land rose into a ridge of hickory, red bay, and black gum trees. Eventually, he thought, when this land belonged to the people, they could clear this drier ground and grow cotton, maybe tobacco as cash crops. For now, it was thick woods with a few trails worn through the wilderness by the Indians.

He heard a rustling in the underbrush and stilled himself. Quietly he eased the rifle off his shoulder, his eyes scanning the brush. Rather than a deer, he saw a man crouched behind a clump of palmetto. "Come on out of there," he said.

The man rose slowly, his body emerging from the palmetto crowns like a great black flower. Justice.

Charles took his time considering. They were only a couple of miles from the quarters, more east than north. Did Justice know freedom lay to the north? Most slaves knew that even if they had no notion which way north was. His hands were empty. No bundle of cornpone to get him through the next days.

"You running?" Charles asked.

Justice walked out from the palmetto thicket clad only in a heavy shirt, his canvas pants tied at the waist with a drawstring, and a pair of thin-soled shoes. No weapon, no food, no blanket. Scouting then.

"Just walking around," Justice said.

The two of them, one black as soot, the other the warmer tone of milky coffee, took each other's measure. Justice looked cold in his shirt. Made Charles appreciate his warm jacket, the wool socks on his feet. But Justice had chosen to be out here in the woods instead of in a cabin with his feet stretched out to the fire.

"Lost?"

"No, I ain't lost," Justice answered, a hint of annoyance in his voice.

"Which way is north?"

Charles watched his eyes, waiting for a flicker of understanding, of deception.

Justice gave nothing away. He held Charles's gaze and tilted his head to the left. "That way."

Charles smiled. He pointed in a direction ninety degrees from Justice's nod. "More like that way."

Charles tipped the rifle over his shoulder again. "What you doing out here?"

"Hunting. Just like you."

"You got no gun."

Justice shrugged. "Possums ain't very fast."

Neither moved to leave, both of them willing to let the silence grow between them. Charles studied the younger man, wondering how to bridge the gap between them, he apparently in the white man's lap, Justice a slave, bitter enough to think of running. Trust would be a risk, for both of them.

"I saw the scars on your back, at the slave market. That many, I figure running is what earned them. How many times you try for it?"

Justice didn't answer. But he didn't deny running either.

"You were smart, you wouldn't have a back full of scars," Charles said. What he wanted was to goad the man into showing himself.

"You got scars on your back?" Justice asked.

Charles smiled again. "No scars."

"But you still a slave."

Charles snorted. "So are you, smart man."

Fire flared in Justice's eyes. He was a runner all right, Charles thought. Willing to risk the lash, or as a repeat runner, more likely some form of mutilation. Andry usually chose ears for a first-time runner brought back half dead from fear and hunger, scratches and bites. Charles had seen a man blown up from mosquito poison, delirious with it. That man, like others who'd faced down a gator, or a nest of moccasins, or spiders creeping into their hair, had wept like a baby to be brought back to the quarters where, even if it cost him his ear, he'd be given clean water, salve for his raw skin, food, a roof, a bed. Brave, and very stubborn, a repeat runner, especially the ones who already knew how dangerous the woods and swamps of Louisiana were.

Charles moved his head in the slightest nod, deciding this was the moment. "Running is not the only way."

He watched Justice think about that. He'd be smart to suspect a trap. If he betrayed an understanding that Charles offered rebellion and showed a spark of enthusiasm for it, he'd know

Charles need only say a word in the master's ear and Justice would be cruelly, mercilessly executed. Yet if the conspiracy were real and he rejected any involvement in it, Charles would have to see to it that he met with an unfortunate, fatal accident.

Justice stared at him, his face expressionless. Finally, he broke eye contact and looked off into the sky. A gray sky today, the clouds shapeless and low. Rain coming, Charles thought. He waited.

Finally, Justice looked back at him. "What you say could get you killed, was I to tell somebody."

Charles watched a pair of squirrels chase each other around a tree. He kept his tone casual. "You plan to tell anybody?"

Justice shook his head.

Answer enough. Charles knew what he needed to know. He'd let the possibilities sink in before he talked to Justice again. He gave the man a nod and turned to head back to his own cabin where he could light a fire and smoke his pipe.

Justice's voice came from behind him. "When?"

Charles raised a hand as he walked on. "Soon."

Chapter Thirteen

Quamana slept soundly the nights after he'd slain two men. He had no second thoughts, no doubts.

There had been one moment only when Quamana's mind flashed on that moment of havoc. He had walked past the empty cabin, Crawley's widow and her children gone from there, and suddenly felt the knife in his hand, the soft resistance of flesh as he plunged the blade into their bodies, the wet heat of their blood on his hands. In his mind, it had been soundless, this taking of life. He remembered only the dark, the knife, and the blood. He blinked his eyes, the impressions vanished, and he was free of them. He had done what needed to be done.

And he had gotten away with it. At the big house, it was beyond Brown's understanding why a slave would rise up and murder a white man. Slave owners everywhere feared revolt, their slaves rising up to slaughter them in their beds, but this was not a revolt. This was one man, and Alphonse, by all accounts, was no trouble maker. The overseer had not singled him out for punishment, had given the slave no reason for resentment. The man had gone mad, that was the only explanation.

In the quarters, Jamaica and Rosa talked to the women, reminding them of how strange Alphonse was. The two or three women who had briefly allowed him into their beds remembered with distaste that he'd been a strange lover, too, inclined to giggles and hasty completion. With every retelling or prompting of memories, the two women reinforced the conviction that Alphonse had taken a knife to the overseer.

So Kook and Jamaica and Rosa—they knew. But everyone else accepted the explanation Brown leapt to. Alphonse had killed Crawley, and Crawley had killed Alphonse. Neither would be missed.

Brown himself had to take on Crawley's job until he could find a new overseer, and what man would eagerly accept a job where his predecessor had been murdered?

The first morning of his new duties, Brown showed up in the bell yard unshaven, bleary eyed, and late. Kook, typically, enjoyed the sight of the usually pristine, proud, strutting master appearing before them with his neck cloth askew and his hair still shaped into tufts by his pillow. Everyone else milled about, murmuring their uneasiness. They could expect nothing good from Crawley's death, not when one of their own had killed him. Not when two hired white men stood at Brown's elbow with rifles.

Quamana exchanged a look with Kook. The master was frightened. They didn't want the white masters frightened. They wanted them comfortable, heedless, and complacent.

Quamana crossed his arms and put his weight on one foot as Brown wiped a hand over his stubbled face and looked like he wanted to say something. What is he thinking? Quamana wondered. *Is one of you planning to kill me, too?*

Brown seemed to gather himself and the moment passed. "It's time to start the winter planting. You niggers finish up hoeing the last three acres today, I'll send a keg of cider down." He fished in his jacket pocket and handed a key to one of his armed guards. "Follow Hank here over to the tool shed and pick up your hoes. I'll be along directly see how you're doing."

Quamana watched his fellow slaves eyeing the man with the rifle. Crawley had worn a pistol at his belt, and a whip, but he hadn't walked around with his gun cocked, ready to shoot.

"Go on, now," Brown said.

They straggled along to the tool shed for rakes and hoes, then moved out to the field. The man called Hank followed them, his gun held loosely under his arm, pointed at the ground, but threatening nonetheless.

People worked all morning with one eye on the guard. When Brown showed up looking like he'd had a meal and several cups of coffee, they kept on hoeing.

"Some of you leave off here and go on down to the drainage ditch," Brown said. "Get the weeds out of there before the next rain."

Quamana kept his head down, watching the others from the corner of his eye. No one counted himself or herself as "some of you." They continued turning the ground over as if the master had not spoken.

Quamana bent to pull a weed and turned his head to watch Brown, and Hank. Brown looked confused. Hank chewed a stalk of grass.

"I said some of you go work on the drainage ditch," Brown said, louder now.

When no one moved to obey, his face reddened. He marched over to Hank, took the rifle from him, and fired it into the sky.

Now everyone's hoe stilled. They turned to look at the master, their faces bland.

Brown pointed with the gun barrel. "You, you, you two, and you—get on in that ditch and clean it out."

Kook, Remo, and four other men hefted their hoes over their shoulder and walked toward the ditch on the edge of the field. And Quamana now knew what he needed to know. Brown was not a man.

Chapter Fourteen

Annique felt slow-witted, like her head was full of clouds. She wanted to sleep all day. Her breasts were tender and swollen. She was pregnant.

She had not known it when she'd asked Charles to jump the broom with her. When he'd walked away from her yet again, when the world became a dark and lonely place, she hadn't been sure then either.

But she knew it now. In the morning, she'd be lethargic like a frog buried in mud, and by afternoon her spirits would soar high as a hawk in the sky. She'd caress her belly, not even swollen yet, and rejoice at the blessing she carried inside her. Yet an hour later, she'd be weeping in despair that Charles had turned from her.

She knew he was different from other men. Like a tortoise, he wore a thick, hard shell to protect him from feelings. But he had them. Those first few weeks, they'd been mad for each other, Charles stealing to her bed early and late, the two of them all hands and mouths and moans. Sometime in those first heated weeks, she began to see the man beneath the shell. He was guarded, afraid of his own vulnerability to feeling and pain, but with every touch and every kiss, she told him that he was safe with her.

And then he'd seen the master leaving her cabin.

Yes, Annique understood why Charles, her proud, complicated love, had run from her. From feeling. And because she understood, she forgave. For a time.

Though she cried and grieved, a spark of anger grew, too. Why did Charles blame her for what the master had done? Didn't other men know the master had had their wives, and learned to live with it? Didn't they love their women anyway? Almighty Charles was too good for her? Too high-toned to do what other men did? Damn him to hell. For all his light skin, his fine ways and manners, Charles Deslondes was a slave, just like her.

The afternoon Annique saw him again, she was toiling outside the laundry house, her jaw set and her lips tight. She scrubbed a blue shirt hard against the washboard, rubbing the dye right out of the collar, working herself into a froth of resentment. Wasn't she better off without him? Of course she was, him a man more stone than flesh and blood. Her baby didn't need a cold-hearted, cold-blooded, heartless daddy, didn't need a man with no more feeling than a piece of shoe leather.

It was as she punished the blue shirt that she caught sight of Charles skirting the laundry yard on the way back from taking some message to her master. If he had come an hour earlier, she might have run to him, her arms open, and begged him to come back to her. But now, instead of sorrow or hope or grief, what she felt was a flare of white hot anger.

"You!" she called.

He stopped. Again he was going to just stand there like a wall. She strode across the yard, her fisted hands trailing soapy water. "You don't walk away from me, not this time you don't."

She stopped two feet away from him, the hair on the back of her neck stiff with anger, her hands on her hips.

"What kind of man are you, Charles Deslondes, to turn away from the woman loves you? From the woman you love, and don't you tell me you don't. But if you so shriveled up inside you can't love me anymore, then you can forget about being a daddy to this baby."

His mouth moved, but nothing came out.

"You heard me. If you can't be a husband, you don't get to be a daddy. So you just get on out of here and don't show your sorry self in my yard again."

Charles stood there stupefied. A baby?

It could be Trepagnier's baby. Desperate for an answer, his mind raced as he tried to calculate. It took only moments for him to realize Annique had the look, some indefinable something, a rounding of her features, a glow. And it had been only eleven days since her master took her. A fine wire thrummed from his head to his toes, vibrating a thin high note. She was not carrying Trepagnier's child. She was carrying his.

"Look at you. You're nothing but a lump of rock, standing there staring at me!"

In the awful moment Annique's rage collapsed into grief, her hands flew to her face, and she fell to her knees.

His hands trembling, he knelt beside her. He touched her. He moved closer and took her shoulders in his hands. She raised her ravaged face to him. He wanted to say he was sorry, he wanted to say he loved her, but the words stuck in his throat.

She threw her arms around his neck and held on tight. He raised her with him and carried her past the laundry house and the smithy and into the quarters. He kicked her cabin door open and kicked it closed behind him.

He sat on the edge of the bed, Annique in his lap, and held her as she sobbed. His mind shut down; he was nothing but pain as the great icy core inside him thawed. With trembling hands he stroked her back, her warmth seeping into him, melting all the hard cold walls he hid behind. He squeezed his eyes shut and tightened his arms around her.

When Annique spent all her tears and quieted, Charles held her still, her head tucked under his chin. The wind rustled through the trees outside, and in the distance he heard the smithy clanging his hammer against the anvil. The cabin smelled of the tansy Annique had hanging from the rafters, of ashes in the grate, of bacon grease.

He couldn't speak, even now. Instead he held her, cherished her, his promise in his arms. When the cabin darkened and grew colder, he pulled the quilt back and lay with her in the bed, his hand on the side of her face, hers fisting the fabric of his shirt.

He had been a fool to think that other mattered. Only this mattered, Annique, here, gazing into his eyes. He wasn't cold anymore, or afraid anymore.

Christmas Day, Charles walked with Annique to the little church, the priest's bell calling everyone to mass. Blue sky, bright sun, a perfect day. Annique, all aglow, wore her treasured calico tignon fastened with a camellia at her temple. Charles had polished his boots and brushed his coat.

During mass, incense sweetening the air, Annique slipped her hand into his and he held on through the recitations, the prayers, the sermon. He needed her touch to tether him, love and hope and this strange ballooning happiness threatening to lift him out of his body. She squeezed his hand and his heart swelled into his throat. Charles was not a praying man, but he closed his eyes and thanked God for this gift, to love and be loved.

After the service, people gathered round them in the churchyard. The priest, his fee a gift from Andry to Charles for the occasion, stood with them, blessed them, and witnessed the ceremony.

Annique's auntie laid the beribboned broom flat on the ground. Charles took Annique's hand and gazed into her smiling face. Together, they made the hop over the broom handle, and everyone rushed forward to kiss them, to wish them well.

Charles couldn't stop smiling. Never in his life had he smiled like this. Mathurin clapped him on the back. George shook his hand. Cooksy grabbed his face and pulled him down for a big sloppy kiss. Little Lydia stood close beside her and dared to dart a quick peck on his cheek. She smiled, and he wrapped an arm around her shoulder and hugged her.

A drum started up and someone joyfully sawed a fiddle. Annique grabbed his arm and pulled him into the dance with everyone they knew, joy asserting itself, insisting on sunshine in Charles' gray and dismal world.

Cooksy organized the food and laid it out on planks, cakes specially made in each plantation's cookhouse, fried chicken, corn bread, pickles. Charles had copied out Bible verses for the Baptist lady down the river, writing the letters big for her failing sight, and from those earnings, he bought a keg of cider for the celebration.

They danced, and they ate, and they laughed. Charles couldn't take his eyes off Annique. He hadn't been happy enough in his life to know what to do with it. He didn't recognize this lightness in his chest, this steady thrum in his ears of a heart pumping with joy instead of dark purpose. He only knew he breathed for her.

Her friends would call her away from him and he would watch her go to them, laughing, chattering, hugging. And he'd see her soon turn from them, searching for him, finding him, and smiling, for him.

He saw Kook and his woman dancing with the others. Did Kook too know this weightless happiness with his woman? He looked around him. Till now, he had only seen their hardship and their frustration and their impotence. Because he had not been fully alive himself, he had been blind to the depth of other people's experience in the world. He thanked God for giving him a taste of this fuller life, of completion, before he died. For the rebellion was not put aside now that he had everything to live for, a woman, a child, love. Not even for them could he abandon this greater purpose. What kind of man would he be, he with all his advantages, if he didn't fight for his people? If he didn't fight for his wife and child to be free?

Standing on the edge of the jostling dancers, Quamana stood like an oak, his arms crossed over his chest, his eyes flat and somber. Charles met his gaze across the yard. Yes, he told him with his eyes. Yes, soon.

Charles ran himself ragged, putting in his day's work on Andry's place, hurrying through the dark to Annique's, then rising early to be back at Andry's for the morning bell. Most nights, she was asleep when he eased into her cabin, letting the cat out and the cold air in. She'd awaken, and he'd climb into bed, into her open arms.

Back in the summertime, in the first weeks he'd come to Annique, he'd been like a wild creature, all heat and fervor. Like no woman before her, she'd been unafraid of his intensity, had matched his energy and fire, and her longed-for reciprocation had unleashed in him a desperate need. He craved a deeper connection, and he had found it with her. No one else had ever wanted true intimacy with Charles. He was too closed off, too hot, too cold. But not for Annique.

Now that edge of loneliness was gone. Simply gone. With Annique in his arms, Charles was at peace. Tired as he was, he'd lie awake in her narrow bed and listen to the world. In all his years, the murmuring fire as it died down to embers, the whisper of wind in the chimney, the solitary sound of his own breathing had reminded him of his isolation. Now the murmuring fire, the whispering wind, and the quiet breathing of his wife beside him, all of these soothed him.

Before Annique, Charles had not understood how a man who suffered the indignities of brute labor might lie down at night with his woman and be consoled. Now he saw how her arms, her love, her recognition that he too was a man, would strengthen him in the night so that he might face another day in bondage.

It was seductive, this tranquility. It made it easier for a man to accept his bonds, easier to accept having his courage trod upon, ground into the dirt, obliterated. It made him weak.

He pulled Annique closer to him and spread his hand over her belly. Hardly a bulge there yet. Did his child's heart beat? Did his child feel the warmth of his hand through his mother's skin? What joy it would be to feel his boy, his girl, move under his hand, to feel an elbow or a knee slide under his palm.

He might not live long enough for that. He might be dead before his child quickened in the womb. But if he died so that his family was free, that was worth his life.

And maybe he wouldn't die. He closed his eyes and slept.

Chapter Fifteen

The last Saturday of the month, as soon as it was dark, Charles left the Andry place and rode down to the Spaniard's tavern where poor whites and slaves could congregate and drink on a Saturday night. Not every slave had permission to or the means to buy a drink, of course, but there were those whose masters hired them out and let them keep a few coins from the wages they brought back. Carpenters and others with special skills mostly, men who'd proven they could be trusted to stay within the master's orbit. Men like Charles, or seemingly like Charles. Few of them had plans to light the world on fire.

Charles tied the reins to a rail and stepped inside the large wood-framed house where the Spaniard had a bar and a few tables set up for his customers to drink crude rum, or, when he had it, crude ratafia. There were maybe a dozen men in the gloomy saloon, their shadows cast on the bare floor by the single lantern hung from the ceiling. The place smelled of rotting boards and cheap tobacco. A man with a fiddle played dolefully in the corner.

Charles glanced around the room. Five of these men were with him. They didn't know that about each other. Charles had structured the conspirators into small circles so that very few knew who was with them and who wasn't. Charles himself did not know every man in his confederacy. Quamana and Kook, Mathurin, Kenner, and Chapin too had formed groups.

He ordered a glass of the wine-based ratafia and grimaced as the first taste burned its way down his throat. "What'd you make this batch out of, Joseph?" he asked the Spaniard. "Cabbage and jalapenos?"

The Spaniard grinned. "It is my secret, amigo. Perhaps you should stick to rum."

"I've had your rum," Charles said and raised his glass of ratafia.

Mathurin came in and joined him at the bar. He gave Charles a searching look, noted that the habitual crease between his brows was eased. And there was something in his eyes.

"Married life agrees with you, my friend."

Charles smiled.

"Rum," Mathurin told Joseph the Spaniard.

When it came, he tipped his head and swallowed it in one go.

"It's that good, eh?" Joseph said and laughed.

Mathurin blinked his eyes and tapped his chest. "Ahh," he gasped.

Charles slapped his back. "Come on."

The two went into the night and down the river road a hundred paces. There was only a quarter moon, but they moved under a tree into the deepest shadows before they spoke.

"What news from New Orleans?" Charles asked.

"Chapin sent word with Tinker." Tinker, an itinerate freed man who ranged from New Orleans to Baton Rouge mending pans and kettles, had bought his own freedom, but his wife and daughters still slaved for Jean Noël Destrehan. "Word is West Florida is in anarchy. Tinker heard a Pensacola trader say the Spanish are on their way from Havana to retake the territory. Said there's piracy on the Pascagoula, too. The governor will hear the same news."

"Chapin thinks Claiborn means to send his men into Florida territory?"

Mathurin nodded. "The suttlers are laying in provisions, buying up wagons. Tinker says they'll be moving out soon."

They stood in the dark, listening to the murmur of the river just beyond the levee.

"Charles," Mathurin said. "What are we waiting for?"

Charles had told no one, not even Mathurin or Kenner, the timetable in his head. But the time was near. Mathurin needed to know.

"I keep a journal. An almanac. When the purple martins arrive, and the waxwings. The phases of the moon. The height of the river. Rainfall."

Mathurin waited for more.

"It's rained the third week in January for the last six years. Every year."

"I don't understand. I thought when Carnival arrived, we'd ––
"

"Epiphany comes early this year. Carnival goes on for weeks after that. The whites will still be partying when the rains come."

"Rain. How will that help us? It'll be just as hard for us to get around as it will be for the whites."

"No. We'll be on foot, most of us. They've got the ladies to think of, and carriages, and they'll be in flight. We work outdoors year around. The weather won't stop us. And they won't be able to call for help in the rain, won't be able to see us or hear us when we come."

Mathurin's voice carried all his hope, and not a little reverence for the heavy significance of what they did. They would make history. "Three weeks. Maybe less."

"The rain doesn't follow my timetable. Keep it to yourself."

"Yes, yes, I will."

Sunday afternoon, Charles sat in Annique's cabin eating her grits and bacon. She sat across from him, watching him stir molasses into the grits. "You're not eating?" he said.

Her smiles these days were radiant and he found his own face warming with the pleasure of it.

"I'm just waiting to see how much of that molasses you gone pour on your plate. You eat like a child, Charles Deslondes."

He reached across the table and poured a puddle in the middle of her grits. "Eat up. You're going to need your strength," he said and waggled a brow at her.

She laughed. He grinned. Charles had sketched out a calendar. Maybe fifteen more days living in this cabin, loving Annique, feeling the baby grow under his palm. Fifteen more days of life, and he told God every day how grateful he was for these weeks before he turned their world on its head.

He cocked an ear. Drums had started up. It sounded like it came from the Brown plantation, Kook and Quamana's place, the next one upriver from Trépagnier's where they sat over their dinner.

The cadences began to fall into a pattern of phrases. Someone was calling for a meeting. Tonight. In the forest. It had to be Mathurin. Many slaves could read the drums, but only he and

Mathurin, Quamana and Kook knew these particular coded drumbeats. They'd worked them out more than a year ago, the four of them.

"Charles, you reading the drums? What do they say?"

He listened to the rest of the messages. "Somebody jumped the broom today. Everybody's invited."

"Let's go!" Annique said. "Let's dance till we can't dance no more."

He reached across the table and stroked her hand. "As long as you don't get overtired."

"Never! Not as long as the drums beat."

So many times Charles had wanted to tell Annique what was to come. He'd never had that impulse before. Secrecy came naturally to him, but he wanted to share everything with her, to prepare her. Yet if they failed, she needed to be able to convince the whites that she had known nothing of the plot. So he told her nothing.

They finished their dinner. Annique tied her tignon, and Charles walked her through the back lane to the dance. A strong wind blew, and overhead the sky was free of clouds. Charles told himself it meant nothing. That was only one sign of an impending rain storm. It could be merely a shower passing through, not a storm.

God, let it not be now, he prayed. Let us have these few more weeks.

They joined the celebrations, everyone glad and festive. For a while, Charles gave himself over to the joy of rhythm and movement, of Annique's delight and happy face. Then Charles saw Kook in a circle of men. There was no hint of the smiling, happy-go-lucky Kook Charles had distrusted. His face was somber as he shuffled, leapt, and charged in mock battle with the others. Some of these men had been warriors. Some of them would follow Kook on the day of reckoning.

And outside the dance, looking on, stood Quamana. Beside him was the woman Jamaica, the one who had helped him the night he killed the overseer. The two of them were tall, well-made, in their prime, and they stood like sentinels of doom. The woman had nothing else to lose in this life, Mathurin had argued, and she'd made herself an accomplice to Crawley's murder. So she was now one of them.

As the sun lowered, Mathurin appeared at Quamana's elbow. Soon Kook broke away from the dance and joined them.

Charles angled Annique out of the dance. "I have a little business before supper. Let me walk you home, and I'll come back in a while."

"What kind of business you got on a Sunday afternoon?" she asked.

"Andry wants to log some timber from Trouard's place, and his man Mathurin is here." He held her hand as they took the lane running the few hundred yards between the dance here at Brown's and Annique's cabin at Trépagnier's. "I won't be long. What you got for supper?"

"What do you care? All you gone do is drown it in molasses."

He put his arm around her shoulder and slid into the familiar duality of his life. He walked Annique through the gloaming, his fingers aware of the shape of her shoulder, the warmth of her skin. He laughed with her about her cat bringing in a mouse as a present, smelled the scent of her rising up from her heated flesh. And he dreaded the coming meet with Mathurin. He expected trouble, Quamana and Kook pushing, always pushing to act now. Now.

At her door, he pulled her to him and kissed her deeply, his hand roving down to her bottom. She leaned into him and said, "You sure you got to talk to that man tonight?"

He bit her neck and opened the door for her. "I'll be back quick as I can, you can count on it."

It was nearly full dark, and he strode into the night for the clearing in the woods. The three men were there ahead of him. The woman Jamaica was not with them. Good. The fewer people who knew the details of their plans, the better.

In the distance, Charles could still hear the drums, the youngsters prolonging the dance as long as their elders would let them.

The shutter on Mathurin's dark lantern was nearly closed, the dim rays of light playing around his feet. Mathurin and Kook sat on a log, Charles and Quamana stood.

Charles waited. This meeting was irregular and risky. Let them explain themselves.

It was Quamana who spoke first. "The governor moves the troops out of New Orleans. Carnival starts in a few days. It is time to act, yet you do nothing."

Kook raised himself from the log and stood beside his friend. "We are tired of waiting. It's time."

Charles, his arms crossed over his chest, said, "It is not time."

"I have not told them," Mathurin said.

The light coming from below Kook's chin showed a face as grim as any expression Quamana ever wore. A dangerous man, Kook, Charles had come to understand.

"We do not need you to begin this thing," Kook said.

Charles felt the anger rise in him like a hot flood. Kook knew nothing. Quamana knew nothing. They were warriors only. They had not planned this from the beginning, had not analyzed every plantation between here and New Orleans. They did not know where to find the keys to every store room and armory, who they could count on, who they must beware of. They had not thought through every eventuality. They had not recruited, trained—

"You need to trust them, Charles," Mathurin said.

Charles's spine was stiff and his arms tensed. He willed himself to loosen his muscles. He dropped his arms and opened his hands. They were so close now. They could not afford to fall out among themselves.

"You, Quamana. Have you made plans for the days after the revolt? Who will direct the spring planting? Free or not, people have to eat." Charles kept his voice calm as if he were merely asking reasonable questions, not pointing out to these two that they knew nothing. "You, Kook. Will there be a council? Who will lead it? Will you divide the land among our people, or will you farm as one community? Will you have a cash crop, and how will you market it? What have you planned to do with the whites? Ask them to please leave? Will you form a militia?" And finally, "Who will lead our people if you, Kook, you, Quamana, all four of us are dead?"

Even in the faint light, he could see Kook's stance soften, but Quamana remained stiff.

"It is time," the big man said as if Charles had not spoken.

"Soon."

Quamana seemed to swell in the lantern light. Mathurin rose and put his hand on Quamana's arm.

"Tell them, Charles. They need to know. They need to be able to reassure the others."

After a moment, Charles nodded.

"For the last six years, the third week in January has been wet. A front moves through and we get rain. Sometimes lots of it. The rain will be our shield. They won't hear us. They won't see us. And they can't run from us."

Neither of his heated co-conspirators spoke.

"I know where every musket is. I know where the powder is and how to load the gun. I know where the machetes are and how many men we have at each plantation. I have communication with New Orleans. You do this before time, you lose all that." He stared at their shadowy faces, bore in on their dark eyes. "We have never had a better chance. You will not destroy this rebellion. You will wait."

Not a bird rustled in the bushes, nor a raccoon, nor a squirrel. The world was silent around the four men. Charles poised, aware of the knife at his back and the other in his boot. These two were younger and bigger, but they knew nothing. They would wait, or they would die.

"Until the rains, then," Kook said.

Chapter Sixteen

Every morning that Charles woke with Annique pressed against him, he'd count down one more day. He tried to ignore the passing of the days, tried to live in this moment, to focus on the joy of having her in his arms. But he'd had no practice at being mindful of the simple pleasures in life, of accepting happiness. Instead, he tightened his arms around her, a lump in his throat. Twelve more days, perhaps, until the rains came.

He pressed his hand lightly against Annique's growing belly, wishing his little one would kick or roll over, but it was too soon. Feeling the life he and his beloved had made was a joy he might never have. But the child would be born, would be his, and if he could make it happen, his son or daughter would be free.

After a quick breakfast, he kissed Annique goodbye and rode down the lane back to Andry's. Last night, there had been a glow around the quarter moon, but he'd told himself it was a faint ring. Now the rich smell of turned-over earth rose from the ground. The cows, instead of grazing in their pasture, lay with their front legs folded, chewing their cud. He searched the sky, dread rising in him.

A troop of swallows swooped low preying on insects. He'd noted it in his almanac over the years. The cows, the rising scent of the earth, the moon. And the swallows flying low.

He and Annique wouldn't have twelve more days. The rain was coming.

Charles worked the morning at the sawmill site digging post holes for the ten-inch foundation piers. If they managed six of them today, he'd count it a good day's work—not for Andry, but for themselves. Before the mill was finished, it would belong to all of them, part of Charles' plan to finance their new beginning. He meant for them to cut back on the brutal cane farming, so they'd need to cut timber for cash. There'd always be plenty of food growing in these fields, but they needed more than food to prosper.

When he looked up, there stood Gilbert Andry next to his fine horse, the reins in his hand. Charles himself stank, probably had dirt on his face, certainly on his shirt and pants, and there posed Master Gilbert in all his pretty clothes and delicate lace. Charles felt at no disadvantage. The pretty man couldn't work, couldn't think, if past behavior was any measure. He had no self-respect or he wouldn't be hanging around Charles and tittering at his own lewd jests.

"Mr. Gilbert," Charles said and eyed the shine on the man's boots. Some other man, maybe one of these slaves working on the posts, would soon be wearing them.

Charles had worked up a sweat and opened his shirt to the waist. That's where Gilbert's eyes lit, on his bared chest and ribs. Charles's skin crawled.

"Why are you knee deep in muck, Charles?" Gilbert waved a lace-edged handkerchief under his nose, the lavender scent wafting over the fecund black earth. "You're supposed to manage, not do the work yourself."

Charles eyed the trunk they were maneuvering into the hole. It was ten feet tall, probably weighed more than a horse. How few men did Gilbert suppose would be enough to handle a job like this? He didn't see any point in explaining.

"I hear you're a married man," Gilbert said. "Is she—"

"Hold. Hold!" George urged as the trunk tilted too far.

Charles turned back to lend his shoulder and didn't bother to notice whether Gilbert stayed to watch the show.

Once the crew got the second post in, righted, and stabilized, Charles called a rest. He walked over to the water bucket and ladled up a drink, then shivered as the winter air cooled his sweaty skin. He could hear a commotion on the other side of the smithy and supposed he should go see about it, but he'd rather sit down for five minutes. When he heard a horse whinny, though, he knew he'd better get over there. The only horse about on the place today was Gilbert's.

He trotted over, dreading whatever mischief Gilbert was up to this time. He rounded the blacksmith shed and saw Maisy with her hands at her face, crying, and little Betsy Marie, George's oldest girl, running scared between the smithy and the rail fence, back and forth, the big horse herding her like she was a calf in a pen. Gilbert's face was alight with the fun, his grin showing white teeth and a streak of meanness wider than the Mississippi. Betsy Marie's eyes were big as saucers.

Charles sprinted for the girl, pushing right under the roan's chest to grab her up and swing her over the rails to safety. He whirled back to the horse, rearing now, its hooves flashing over his head.

Charles dodged the hooves and grabbed for the reins. Furious as he was, he still had to manage the fool in the saddle. As if his first thought was for the fool's welfare, he called out, "You hold on, Mr. Gilbert!"

He settled the horse and patted its neck, then looked up at Andry's son with as earnest an expression as he could manufacture. "Don't worry about the girl. I'll see she's punished for spooking your mount."

Gilbert turned red in the face and glared at the girl watching him from the other side of the fence. "Ungrateful little bitch," he muttered, but Charles caught it. So Gilbert had been after Betsy Marie, who couldn't be much more than twelve. He glanced over at her slim form just beginning to show little breasts beneath her cotton dress.

"You take care, Mr. Gilbert," Charles said. He crossed over the fence in one fluid move and took Betsy Marie by the arm. "I'll make sure she won't bother you again," he said, putting some menace behind the threat as he hauled her toward the quarters.

"She deserves a thrashing, running out in front of my horse like that," Gilbert called behind him and rode on, stiff-backed, embarrassed enough for one day, Charles hoped.

Maisy trotted along behind as he strode through the bare pecan orchard, Betsy Marie in tow. "Wadn't her fault," Maisy panted. "She a good girl, but that boy keep on after her."

"He's not a boy, Maisy."

"I know it, and I ashamed it was me raised him up, he turn out so bad."

When they reached the lane running between the cabins, Charles let go of Betsy Marie's arm. He patted her shoulder and looked at old Maisy. "I know it's not her fault. He's after her, though?"

"He is that, and her not even a woman, she just a girl."

"I been fast, Mr. Charles," Betsy Marie said. "He ain't got me, but he be powerful mad when I get away from him."

Charles looked at Betsy Marie's unblemished cheek. Maybe he could at least save George's girl from Celine's fate, a white baby in her belly and a scar on her face. "Your papa know about this?"

Betsy Marie studied the toe of her shoe and didn't answer. Young as she was, Charles saw, she already knew that her father, a man with broad shoulders and the respect of all the other slaves, even he had no power to protect her against a white man.

Charles glanced at the sky. No clouds, but a strong wind from the west. Very soon, Betsy Marie wouldn't need protection from Gilbert Andry. Between now and the reckoning, however, he could do a lot of damage to a young girl. Charles heaved out a sigh and looked at Maisy. "The hogs?"

"Yeah. That be best."

"All right. Betsy Marie, I want you tending the hogs from morning to night, even if they don't need tending. Won't be long you smell like a pig sty, and that'll be all the protection you need."

Betsy Marie, who five minutes before had been a frightened child, lit the whole lane with her smile. "I like pigs just fine, Mr. Charles."

Late in the afternoon, the drums started. Charles lifted his share of another heavy log and helped tilt it into the last post hole as if the beats echoing through the trees and over the fields were no more than another celebration, maybe to rejoice in a child being born in the quarters down at the Brown's or Trepagnier's. He strained to hear, to listen, over the grunts and weary sighs of satisfaction from his crew.

Not everyone could make the drums talk. Not everyone could understand their language. But Charles knew the patterns, the familiar phrases, the rise and fall of tone, the changes of rhythm or tempo. "Rain is coming," the drums said.

Chapter Seventeen

Quamana, laboring nearby as they stacked wood on the sledge, stopped and rotated his left shoulder like it ached. Kook too felt the changing weather in his bones.

He considered the sky. The morning had been clear, but now the clouds overhead crossed paths, layers being shoved by the dark line to the west. The clouds didn't read Charles's almanac before they moved. Was this the big rain he expected, a week or ten days before mid-month?

He and Quamana trudged through the yard pulling the firewood sled. They passed the corral where the stable boys had turned the horses out in order to muck their stalls. A hollow feeling rose in Kook's gut. The horses were crowded together, facing west. A storm on the way, not just a rain.

It was time.

He straightened when he heard the drums. Quamana looked at him. They listened, their eyes turned to the south where the sound came from. From how far south they couldn't tell, maybe all the way from New Orleans, relayed from one drummer to the next up the river road.

And all the drummers had to say, over and over, was that it was going to rain?

Then the rhythm shifted, a dance beat filled the air, then the rhythm shifted again. Trouble in the city. Kook looked over his shoulder to be certain the slaves plucking chickens for the master's supper wouldn't hear him. "Spanish are coming?" he whispered. "From Cuba?"

Quamana nodded. "They want Florida back."

"There. What was that phrase? Do you know it?"

Quamana listened to the repetition. "Governor is moving troops."

A gust of wind carried the scent of rain. Kook stared at Quamana. "It's time, isn't it?"

Quamana stepped closer and murmured. "I'll finish here. Take Rosie and the children to the maroons."

Kook had waited for this, planned for it, lusted for it, and now that it was here, his heart rose into his throat. He might never see Joshua again, or little Lila. How could he say goodbye to Rosie?

Quamana's voice roughened. "Go on," he commanded.

Fat heavy rain drops plopped on his shoulders as Kook forced himself to merely amble when he wanted to run. He found Rosie feeding the turkeys penned up behind the chicken yard.

She froze when she saw him, her hand in a bag of corn. She knew as well as he did what these wet gusts meant. She'd been waiting as he had, she'd planned as he had, wanting their children to live free. But now? Today? He saw the fear in her eyes and squelched his own. He knew what she needed from him.

He angled his head toward the quarters. She opened the bag of kernels, emptied them on the ground, then pushed her way through the turkeys crowding around her, pecking and pecking.

Kook walked ahead of her, his pulse fluttering in his arteries. He had not expected this fear. Was he not a man? Was he not a warrior? Was he not ready?

He gave his head a little shake. Yes. He was all those things. But grief shook him, too, at what he might lose. The children. Rosie. The sky and the water and the air he breathed.

He went into their cabin to gather what he could while Rosie went to Serafina's to make some excuse for taking her babies early. He collected what food they had in the house, Rosie's cook knife, the spoons, every stitch of clothing, all of it fitting into one burlap bag.

Rosie came in with the children. She didn't look at him. Her gaze roamed over the home she'd made with him, with their babies. This is what Kook could never make Quamana understand. They were slaves, they were poor, they were burdened – and they were angry – but they'd known joy in these four walls.

Kook watched Joshua crawl under the bed after his favorite toy, a top Quamana had made him.

"We can't go till it's dark," Rosie said.

Kook didn't trust himself to keep on the path in the dark. "We go now," he said.

He swept Joshua into his arms, unable to wait another moment, panic nipping at him. Rosie cloaked one of their two quilts over Kook's shoulders and tucked it in around Joshua. Then she wrapped Lila in a shawl across her breast and Kook draped the second quilt over her head and shoulders.

With a last look at her home, Rosie crossed the threshold and Kook closed the door behind them.

It was raining now, the sky low and dark. Rosie shielded Lila's face with her hand, all of them drenched before they left the quarters.

Kook scanned the lane and the fields. Everyone had retreated into their cabins before the rains came down. They'd closed their shutters against the cold wind and the wet. They'd lit their candles and stoked their fires. No one saw him taking his family through the rain and into the forest.

The wind blew sideways into their faces. Thunder boomed as lightning forked across the sky. Kook doubled the quilt around Joshua, protecting him from the worst of the stinging rain and chilling wind, trusting the heat of his own chest would keep his boy warm. Underfoot, the ground could not soak up the water fast enough and they sloshed through deepening puddles. Kook set the pace as fast as Rosie could go, the first part of their trek familiar. What would the trail be like further on where streams would be rushing and overflowing their banks? Where quick sand would be hidden by the rain? Fear threatened him already, and he could not contemplate the horror of Rosie sinking into the earth and him helpless to save her. What if it were he who stepped into the mire and sank inexorably into the sand? He would toss Josh to Rosie and yell at them to go back, back to their cabin where they could light a fire, where they could be safe. He shoved the thought aside and pushed on.

Cold rainwater filled Kook's shoes, then rose to his ankles. He continually checked to see Rosie was right behind him. She splashed through the muck with her head down, her arms sheltering Lila under the quilt.

The rain increased so that Kook could see no more than ten feet ahead until the next flash of lightning lit the way. The bushes along the path lashed at them, tossed by gusting winds and sheeting rain. He shivered in spite of the pace. If the rain slowed down, all this water would skim over with ice. He'd heard that it even snowed in Louisiana some years, but he couldn't imagine being colder than he was right now.

They trudged deeper into the woods behind the plantation. Bushes closed in on them, narrowing the path. The sky darkened with black clouds, the rain sluiced over their feet. He prayed the maroons had heard the drums and would send a group in to learn the last minute details of the plan. He prayed that someone from that party would guide them safely back to their camp where Rosie and the children could get warm and dry. Where they would be far away when the bloodshed started. For there would be blood. Kook himself meant to spill as much white blood as his knife could free from mortal flesh.

He halted. Rosie had fallen behind a dozen feet, too far. When she caught up to him, he turned his back to the wind to shelter her and tipped her face up. Her lips were white with cold and she shivered so hard he could see the sodden quilt quivering.

"Is it much further?" she asked.

"No," he lied. "We'll make it before dark." But the sun was blotted out behind the clouds, and it felt like twilight now, hours before sunset. He slipped his hand inside the quilt, inside the shawl to feel little Lila. She was sound asleep, warm enough against Rosie's breast. "Stay close," he told Rosie and drove on through the darkening woods.

A creek cut across the path, running fast. Kook eased in, gauging the depth and the current. In the middle it came no higher than his thigh. He held out his hand for Rosie, and together they stepped through the rushing water, careful of their footing. When they emerged, Rosie's teeth chattered over the sound of the rain splattering through the trees, pelting leaves and branches and ground.

Kook pushed on, his gut clenched against the fear. What if he got them lost out here in the rain? Rising water and deepening mud obscured the trail. Kook's fatigue further confused the path. Nothing about the clumps of palmetto or the leathery-leaved magnolias seemed familiar. He couldn't build a fire, he couldn't keep them warm, and as dark as it was now, the temperature would drop even further when the sun set. Maybe they should turn back while he still had his bearings. He faltered, and Rosie bumped into him.

He turned. Rain streamed over Rosie's face. Her whole body trembled with the cold.

"Let me see Joshua," she said.

Kook shifted the boy's weight. Cocooned in the soaking quilt, he was awake, his eyes somber and calm even in the midst of the tempest.

Rosie had nursed Lila even as they walked, and she slept. But her skin was so cold when Kook ran a finger over her cheek.

"She's all right," Rosie said. "I feel her warm where she touches my skin."

"We could turn back."

She shook her head. "No. We go on."

They slogged on through quagmires and pools, half-blinded by the lashing rain. Then they entered a clearing where two old trees leaned into each other and Kook knew they were on the right track.

Another hour. The mud was over his ankles and crawling up his shins. Rosie's steps dragged. He took her arm and helped her along where the path allowed it. How long had they walked, how far had they come? Kook pushed the fear for his Rosie and his babies to some dark corner. He tried to make his mind blank, to simply endure.

The little light that filtered through the clouds, the rain, and the trees was fading. He tightened his grip on Rosie's arm and pulled her along as fast as he dared in the gathering gloom. They could not survive a night out here in the cold, the rain and the wind stealing the warmth from their bodies.

"Kook," Rosie shouted over the storm. "Kook, stop."

"We can't stop."

"I can't breathe, Kook. Go on ahead. Find help. I'll wait here."

Where was here? He would never find her again in this forest, in the dark, in the lashing rain. Never.

"We stay together," he said, and tugged her on. They stumbled, they staggered. Kook couldn't feel his toes anymore, nor his fingers. He hugged Joshua, willing his body heat to envelop his son.

Full dark was on them. They flailed blindly, feeling their way with their feet finding open ground, their arms groping for open air.

And there, ahead, glimmers of light. Kook's heart bounced in his chest. They were here. They were saved.

Together they dashed through the clearing to the nearest cabin, a sliver of light slipping under the door and into the night.

Kook pounded on the door, leaning into it, frantic to be let in with his babies, his wife.

The door flew back and he stumbled in, Rosie's arm still gripped in his hand.

He took in the surprised faces, the dismay, and then the quick determination to act. The door shut out the storm. Hands slid the sodden quilts from their shoulders. Other hands took the children to the fire and pulled the wet clothes off their bodies.

Rosie fell to her knees. He knelt beside her and took her in his arms. "You're safe now. You and the children, you'll be safe here."

"Go get Big Tom," somebody said, and the door opened to the wind and slashing rain again.

"Take those wet things off," a woman said and with sure hands pulled at their clothes, blankets at the ready to wrap them in. "Come over to the fire. Sally, heat some water."

When Lila fretted, Rosie held her arms out for her and put her to the breast. Joshua still shivered, but he stuck his thumb in his mouth and leaned into the old woman who held him close and rubbed his feet.

Only now did Kook recognize his host, Big Tom's older son, Ezra, as he came back into the cabin leading his father, both of them dripping water onto the bare floor.

"So it's you," Big Tom said.

Kook accepted a cup of hot water smelling of lemons and molasses. He nodded at the leader of the maroons.

Big Tom sat on the floor, yielding the reach of the fire's warmth to Kook and his family. "You a little crazy coming through the woods a night like this."

Kook cradled the warm cup in his hands and sipped the sweet concoction. He could feel his toes and fingers again. Rosie's shivering had stopped, Lila suckled, and Joshua drowsed before the fire.

"You heard the drums," Kook said.

Big Tom snorted. "The ones said, 'Rain is coming'? We didn't need the drums to tell us that. What we waiting to hear is this." He tapped a pattern on his massive thigh, the exact pattern Kook had taught them when he'd been here before.

"That is what the next drums will say."

"When?" Ezra said.

"Tomorrow. It's time."

"In this storm?" Ezra asked.

"We'll use the storm. The whites will be holed up in their houses, drinking and sleeping through the storm."

"Then we go tomorrow," Big Tom said.

"We leave now, we could be there by morning," said Ezra.

Big Tom stared at the fire, thinking. It was cold, as cold a January as they'd had in years. And the storm showed no signs of letting up. "We go out in this, we'd be lost, cold and dead by morning. We wait for light."

"At dawn, I go back," Kook said.

Big Tom nodded. He raised his big body. "I'll send more firewood over," he said to Ezra who stood scowling with his arms crossed over his chest.

Ezra's wife, half-grown daughter, and the granny arranged the cabin for Kook and his family to sleep on pallets before the fire. They used one of the sodden quilts to block the draft under the door and the other to cover the window where the wind and rain beat under the sash.

Ezra blew out the candle. The storm raged on, but inside, the cabin quieted. Kook lay with Rosie, Josh and Lila between them. He reached over the sleeping children to finger Rosie's hair, still wet and tangled. Around them, Ezra and his family breathed softly and evenly. The fire crackled, burning fiercely with the extra wood Big Tom had sent over to warm them.

Rosie took his hand and held it to her cheek. He felt her grip loosen as she yielded to exhaustion and slept.

Kook dozed fitfully as the wind beat on the ramshackle cabin, finding its way up the cracks in the floor, through the chinks in the walls. He woke up with a cold draft on his back, but the children seemed warm between them. He could see his beloved Rosie's face in the dying firelight, the mouth ever ready with a smile, the cheek smooth and brown. Afterwards, she might be alone in the world. Maybe some other man would love her, would take care of her and the babies. Maybe she would have to do it all alone. She could do that, she was strong of heart, but he didn't want her to have to.

He eased over the children to lie beside his Rosie and take her in his arms. She turned into him and quietly, desperately, they made love in the dying light.

Chapter Eighteen

While Kook was struggling through the storm to get his family to safety, Quamana trudged through the freezing night, rain lashing his face, his way lit only by lightning flashes. Soaked and shivering, he slipped into the warmth of Charles's cabin. Other men were there before him, all of them here for their last instructions. When they met again, they would be armed and at war.

Charles had sent for his lieutenants from downriver, eleven men, by Quamana's count. Some were Africans seized in Kongo and Senegambia and Sierra Leone as he and Kook had been taken from the Asante kingdom. Others had been sold from tobacco plantations in the American states. Slogging through the frigid rain, they had come here tonight from the Trouard plantation, from Trepagnier's, La Branche's, Bernoudy's, Destrehan's. Even Harry was here from the Kenner plantation.

Quamana eyed these men. He did not know all of them. Charles had not meant for them to know one another. Each of them accepted the risks. If they failed, the whites would torture them. They would cut their heads off and hang them on pikes.

In his other life in the Asante Akanland, around the campfires the night before they were to attack the enemy, some of the young ones would laugh too loud, would sing and dance. That was merely fear. The seasoned Akan warriors sat comfortably around their fires, calm and composed. These men in Charles Deslondes' cabin had waited months, some of them years, for this chance. In each of them he saw a determined glow, a steady gaze, and a quiet self-possession. They were not afraid.

Charles stood before the fireplace and all eyes turned to him. "It is time. We are ready." He looked around the room at each face, lingering on the scars that proved Quamana was a warrior. He gave a slight nod, and Quamana accepted the acknowledgement. Charles needed his experience and leadership to guide those slaves who, in spite of a life of injustice heaped on cruelty, had never committed an act of violence before. Quamana, and Kook, and others further down the river, knew weapons, and violence, and blood.

Charles said they could expect twenty-five from his place then called on each man for an account of his group of rebels. Mathurin assured them of ten, Kentuck promised a dozen.

Quamana did not need to hear these numbers. They would be what they would be. Enough, or not enough. He watched instead of listened, and he saw all eyes on Charles Deslondes. They listened to him. They trusted him. Quamana had been right. Charles was the heart of this rebellion. He had forged their dreams of freedom into a force with purpose and direction. He had planned, instigated, and shaped a secret organization. He had inspired loyalty and enforced patience. This man was the father of their new country.

"The goal is New Orleans," Charles told them, his voice carrying over the lashing rain and wind. "Once we hold the port, we will hold all of southern Louisiana. We will be unstoppable!"

Quamana had not seen Charles like this. He'd only seen the taciturn, crusty conspirator speaking softly in shadowed glens. This man was afire.

"Governor Claiborn has moved his soldiers, even the dragoons, eastward to fight the Spanish and settle the territory. The city is undefended."

Charles's eyes burned into every man in the room, kindling their spirits to the sparking point. "The city is ours!"

Thousands, Quamana thought, would follow this man, no matter the risk. He looked around the room, every man's face alight, every man's eye on their leader. He, too, believed, seeing Charles like this, seeing his effect on hard men. This time tomorrow night, they would have struck their first blows. They would have declared themselves free men.

"Mathurin," Charles said, "when we reach — "

A blast like a thousand lightning bolts shook the cabin and forced white light through every chink in the walls and floor. Quamana rushed to the window and threw aside the shutter. A splintered pecan tree fifty yards from the cabin flamed like a giant torch, the bare branches stretching up in blue and yellow fire. Torrents of rain did nothing to dampen the raging flames.

Quamana smiled as he pulled back to let the others see what fire could do. Tomorrow night, they would be just such a power, a strike of lightning that would sear the world.

Mid-day, Quamana had already sharpened his knives. He'd even filed his thumb nail into a weapon as sharp as a spear point. Now he sat in Kook's cabin, his elbows on his knees, his heel tapping against the floor. He made himself be still. Kook was no fool. He'd make it.

The door flung open and the storm pushed in, propelling Kook in a whirl of wind and rain. Quamana caught him before he fell and dragged him to the fire. Mud caked his legs, his skin was ashen, and shivering shook his whole body.

Quamana stripped him of his wet clothes, pulled off his own shirt and rubbed Kook dry.

"Lost my shoes," Kook stuttered.

"You can wear Alphonse's."

Kook's teeth chattered and his trembling grew violent.

"Stay at the fire," Quamana said. He rushed to Jamaica's cabin then went to his own cabin for clothes and a quilt.

Kook lay on his side on the floor curled up, his whole body shaking. Quamana wrapped both of them in the quilt and held on. Jamaica came in with a steaming kettle and a bowl. She poured hot water into molasses and spooned it into Kook's quivering mouth.

"Get the rest of that in him," she said. She poured hot water into a basin and washed Kook's feet while more water heated over the fire.

"Rosie and the children?" Quamana asked.

A great sigh shuddered through Kook. "Safe," he said.

"Get warm. Rest. We do this tonight."

Charles directed that the drums beat all that Epiphany Sunday. The messages flying up and down the river would be hidden in the greater din, the whites thinking it was just another foolish nigger thing--beat the drums, scare the lightning away. Because the lightning in this storm exceeded anything he'd ever seen, flashes and booms and searing streaks across the sky, for hours on end.

When Charles knocked on the outer door of Andry's study, he heard Andry's muffled "Come" through the door. The room reeked of cigar smoke, brandy, and wet wool. Andry lounged in his easy chair and Charles, mindful of his muddy wet boots, stood just inside the closed door, rain dripping off his slicker.

"Everything is fastened down, closed up, Mr. Andry. The horses and mules are snug in the barn, the stores as dry as can be. I've got a man at Black Creek keeping an eye out and another two on the levee."

From the rest of the house, Charles heard the slaves bustling, getting the house ready for the first days of Carnival. As Andry blew smoke and narrowed his eyes at the resulting ring, Charles took the opportunity to glance at the clock. That's why he'd really come, to see the time.

Ten minutes till two o'clock. Time enough to see Annique.

"We'll have to replant the turnips and the collards. Fortunately, the cane shoots weren't in yet," Charles said. Andry didn't seem particularly interested in the cane, the source of all his wealth and comfort. He blew another smoke ring and admired its drift across the room. "They'd be drowned by now," Charles went on, "but they're put up safe. Soon as the fields drain off in a few days, we'll start planting."

"Good man. I'm sure you have it all in hand."

"Yes, sir." Charles let himself out and strode to the back lane, but it had become a stream with rainwater running for lower ground. He kept to the fields, stepping from row to row, stopping now and then to scrape the accumulating mud off his boots.

The chinaberry tree drooped over Annique's roof with the weight of so much rain. He left his boots on the porch and before he could reach for the door catch, she opened the door just enough for him to slide in then slammed it shut against the wind. The next instant she was on him, her arms wrapped around his neck, her mouth pressed to his.

He rocked her as she held on to him, waiting for her to notice she was now soaked all up and down her front. He'd have to take those wet things off her.

"I could eat you up, Charles Deslondes."

He licked her nose to make her laugh, then started on the buttons down the front of her dress.

"You got me wet," she said.

"That's why we're getting you out of this dress. So you won't catch a chill."

She rounded her eyes. "Is that why?"

"The only reason."

"Then you better get out of that slicker. And out of those socks, and those pants, and that shirt."

"Yes, ma'am," he said, and kissed her bare shoulder.

Later, they rested on their sides facing each other, her hand in his and pressed to his chest. Outside the storm raged on. Inside, yellow light from the crackling fire bronzed Annique's skin, the oak log scented the air with the comfortable smell of wood smoke. Annique's cat hopped on to the bed and curled up at their feet.

Annique stared into his eyes. No one else ever did that, really looked at him. But even she couldn't see the whole of him, didn't guess the depth of darkness and roiling fury he hid from the world. When it was over, if he still lived to love her, maybe he could be the man she saw.

His gaze wandered over her face, memorizing the curve of her brow, the wide bow of her mouth. They didn't have so many days as he'd hoped. All they had was now. He pushed a loose strand of hair off her cheek and smoothed it back with his palm.

"What are you thinking?" she asked.

That I never thought I would have this. That I never even knew I could feel this. "That I love you. Don't forget it, ever."

"I might. You ought better tell me, let's see, every Sunday. That way I won't forget."

He cupped her face in his hands and kissed her as if he could empty his heart into hers.

When she slept, Charles rounded his palm across her belly one more time and prayed that God bless his child.

He rose and dressed and took a long lingering look at her sleeping peacefully. Then he entered the storm.

He strode into the relentless rain, his mind at peace. For Annique, for their child. For Lydia and Celine, for Maisy and Betsy Marie. For George who wouldn't fight for himself, for all of them, he would burn down this kingdom of corruption. It was what he was born to do.

Chapter Nineteen

Cold rivulets of rain running down his back, Charles led his men through the dark to the shed where Charles himself had locked the tools they used daily. He opened it and lit a lantern to illuminate the rows of machetes, axes, and hoes. For himself, he hefted a hatchet, then stood aside while Caleb, Justice, Jupiter and the others filed in and chose their weapons.

No one spoke as they left the shed and followed Charles to the big house, two dozen men in soaked-wet cotton clothes, squelching through the mud in the cheap, ill-fitting shoes Andry had allotted them at Christmas.

Guiding them through the dark like a beacon on a far shore was the lantern Charles had hung under the gallery eaves just at dusk. As he had expected, no one in the house had noticed it, and now it called them to their destiny.

At the piazza behind the house, Charles pointed to Jupiter and Old Gus, then motioned them toward the brick store room under the raised house. A dozen men followed them to the militia's armory and supplies. To the others, Charles gestured with his chin and they followed him up the exterior double stairs to the living quarters.

Inside, Gilbert and Manuel Andry would hear only the rain pelting the wooden steps, the windows, the roof, the surrounding oak and laurel trees. Still, Charles and his rebels stepped softly as they climbed the outer stairs, their blades glinting wetly in the lantern light. On the gallery, Charles waited while his men gathered. Caleb pushed through the other slaves to stand before him and Charles nodded. He had not forgotten his promise.

Charles ran the scene through his mind. Unlike Kook and Quamana, he didn't lust to murder every white planter on the river. He meant for their new republic to demand respect in the world, to show the Americans, the Spanish, and the French they were a fair, though determined, people. But Gilbert Andry needed to die. And Caleb would see to Gilbert's father.

Charles took the lantern and opened the door leading from the gallery into the dining room. Silently the rebels trailed mud through the house, past the china figurines on the mantle, past the velvet sofa and the crystal decanter on the rosewood table. At the foot of the interior staircase, Charles turned. Every eye was on him, every hand was poised with an axe or a knife or a hoe. They need only climb these stairs, and the Andrys would be theirs. It was begun.

Charles pointed to Caleb and then to the door on the left of the upper landing. Charles would hold his force back until Manuel Andry's door should be breached, and then, he would take Gilbert.

At the signal, Caleb and his troop raced up the stairs, heedless now of the noise they made. Caleb burst through Andry's bedroom door, a wild shriek tearing out of his chest. Andry screamed.

Charles took the stairs three at a time and busted through Gilbert's door. Gilbert sat up in the bed, his mouth open and his eyes staring, paralyzed at the sound of his father's scream and the pounding of feet on the stairs. When Charles raised the lantern, Gilbert said, "Oh Charles, thank God."

And then Charles strode to the bed, and with no more hesitation than he'd show killing a goose, he swung his hatchet.

The reek of blood filled the room as the other rebels, husbands and brothers and fathers of women Gilbert had used, crowded around the bed, hacking and stabbing, years of anger and hatred behind every blow.

Charles felt no anger, no hatred. Just as he would put down a rabid dog, he had put down Gilbert Andry. And now they would take what they needed from the armory beneath the house and march on to New Orleans.

Shouts and screams still came from Andry's room. Charles turned away from the carnage at Gilbert's bed and strode to the landing. Andry, bloodied and torn, hurtled into him and leapt for the staircase. With a heart-stopping war cry, Caleb pursued him with his bloody machete raised.

Charles had seen the three great gashes pouring blood through the tears in Andry's nightshirt. The man would bleed to death, would die in the cold and the rain and the dark. It was enough. "Caleb," he called. "Caleb!"

The young man, as hot as his blood was, turned back at Charles's command.

"The armory," Charles called down to him.

With Gilbert's gore splattered on their clothes and hands and blades, the men thundered down the stairs behind him. In the armory, Charles called, "Take what you need."

The men crowded into the store room and pawed through uniforms and hats, muskets, ammunition, swords, pikes, and pistols. Charles let them choose what they wanted, each man wild-eyed now they had drawn white blood.

Under Charles's approving eye, they scavenged bits and pieces of blue militia uniforms. Uniforms would add an air of legitimacy to their army as they marched down the river gathering recruits.

His motley band filed out armed with all the weaponry they could carry. Charles shrugged into an officer's coat with gleaming braid and tassels, buckled on a saber, and slung a musket over his shoulder. Last, he tucked into his belt the hatchet he'd used to kill Gilbert Andry.

When he reentered the storm, George was waiting for him, holding the reins to Charles's horse. With a pang, Charles realized how much he wanted George with him, how much he wanted a friend by his side.

"George!" he hollered over the din of the storm. "Get a weapon, some clothes from the armory."

George ignored Charles' extended hand. He shook his head.

The two men who'd labored countless hours side by side year after year stared at each other through the rain.

They needed men like George. Charles touched his saber. He could force George to join them.

No, he decided. Not George.

George offered him the reins. "A leader should be on a horse."

Charles mounted and looked down at George. "We need you."

Again George shook his head.

Charles spurred his old quarter horse to the river road, the men falling into ordered ranks behind him.

"On to New Orleans!" he shouted

The rain pelted on, relentless still in this third day of the storm. In places the mud reached their knees and the rebels hauled one another out of the mire.

Hearing the drums under the roar of wind and rain, timid and cautious slaves ran to neighboring quarters to warn their fellows, to hide, to save themselves. Masters and their families ran for their lives. Other slaves who heard the drums surged out of the quarters and out of the big houses to join the insurrection.

As dawn broke, Charles and his swelling army came to plantation homes already ravaged. Doors stood open. Crystal lamps, leather chairs, even silk and satin dresses trailed across the verandahs and yards, plunder the rebels discarded to join the march to New Orleans.

Charles turned in his saddle to survey the sodden men marching through the mud with energy and determination. Some had horses, all had a cane knife or a shotgun or a club. Their heads were held high, their eyes on the goal ahead.

They would not be denied. Charles believed it now.

Through the rain, Charles made out a band on horseback waiting for them. Mathurin, with ten followers. They would have a full complement of cavalry before long.

Mathurin spurred his horse to ride beside him. "Trouard got away," he shouted over the rain. "One of his house slaves got him out, him and his ladies."

"Where are they?" Charles said.

Mathurin shrugged. "In the swamp, hiding."

"Leave them," Charles said. If they started pursuing every white who ran, they'd dilute their force. New Orleans was the goal, not every planter along the way.

On they marched, the drums stirring their blood and rousing their courage. Charles himself felt the thrill of power pump through his veins as his army grew and sunlight seeped through clouds and rain.

"Freedom or Death" they chanted in the morning rain, the hated whites fleeing before them. Charles allowed his rebels to pillage food and boots and clothing from the mansions as long as the main army marched on. The others would catch up to them once they'd got their fill of plunder.

Chapter Twenty

Before the signal came, Quamana waited with Kook, the two of them quietly alert. In the other world, the other life across the ocean, they had spent many nights before battle in just this companionable silence. Kook had been only fifteen then, but already he'd shown himself a man. Other young soldiers had either slept soundly through the night and then been hard to rouse as the army rose in the pre-dawn to take up their arms, or they'd annoyed their elders with pranks and feverish laughter. Kook would sleep a few hours, then waken to sit with Quamana and his seasoned friends as they waited for dawn. They would kill and perhaps be killed when they attacked the enemy, but they were at ease and at peace as they smoked a pipe or merely watched the stars wheel through the sky.

Keeping vigil, Quamana poked at the log, half blackened, half glowing red, so that it collapsed into the fire sending sparks up the chimney. Outside the wind and rain gusted and lashed, whistled and pattered, but inside, the cabin was quiet. Here they were, poised to destroy one world with violence to create another of justice, but for now, they were isolated in this cabin, the moment heavy with both peace and possibility. The moment, Quamana mused with some surprise, was happiness.

Over the storm, Quamana was not at first certain he heard the drums. He opened the window and leaned into the rain to listen. Unmistakably, the drums rolled down the river in the pre-dawn calling them to action.

Quamana's heart thudded as he turned back to Kook. His friend, who these five years had worn the face of the happy slave, the foolish man-child, stood in the middle of the cabin, firelight playing over his scars and tattoos, a fierce and manic grin on his face.

Kook was first out the door, the two of them splitting up to gather their own lieutenants. Here on Brown's plantation, the two of them had forged the single largest collection of rebels. Both of them formidable men, confident, charismatic, they had drawn young men to them, even Kook with his light-hearted demeanor. Anyone keen enough to contemplate rebellion also observed intelligence and power beneath the foolish persona.

They had followed Charles's plan – only the men in each small group knew of one another--but they had created many small bands. Quamana tapped on five doors and was joined by the leader of each of his groups. They in turn assembled their men. Secrecy no longer mattered. The rebels gathered in the cold rain, lanterns revealing who among all the slaves on this plantation dared to rebel.

These were not gangs of impetuous, foolhardy youths. During midnight conferences Quamana and Kook had trained their officers who then inculcated their own small groups with military discipline. Without orders, the recruits arranged themselves into units under their immediate leaders, then all turned to the two African warriors who stood a head taller than most of them, their shoulders broader and stronger, their scars proof of their valor. They would gladly follow Quamana and Kook into a new world.

With a mighty kick, Kook broke the lock on the storage shed. The men crowded in to grab cane knives and hoes and scythes and axes. When Quamana emerged from the shed with his weapons, Jamaica came to him. Wordlessly, he handed her a machete.

Pumping up the young rebels behind him, Kook yodeled a war cry and led the charge to the master's house. He burst in followed by slaves shrieking like wild men. They swiped china figurines to the floor, smashed the ormolu clock, and hacked at the delicate Louis Quatorze tables.

Kook pushed on through the house and discovered the front door swinging open in the wind.

Brown too would have heard the drums. He had escaped. Kook rushed into the storm, peering through the rain and the dark. There! A horse neighed, and harness jangled. He sprinted for the road, his cane knife held high, his war cry curdling the sodden air.

But he could not outrun a horse. Brown thundered away on his mount, disappearing into the rain. Kook drove his blade into the muddy road and cursed in frustration.

He moved back into the house to lead a crew to the storerooms underneath. Remo, the boy who shared Quamana's cabin, began tearing at the sacks of grain, spilling oats onto the puddled floor.

"Stop, you fool!" Kook grabbed the boy's shoulder and whirled him around. "What do you plan to eat next week, Remo, and the week after? Fill your pockets with nuts and raisins, take the rest to the quarters."

Kook raced back up the stairs to gather the men and set the fires that would burn Brown's house to the ground. The rebels, excited that the hated master had run from them, laughed as they rifled through clothes and shoes, pulling on velvets and silks to protect them against the driving rain.

Quamana and Jamaica ran for the stables. They pushed aside the stable boy, an old man who had lived his whole life as Brown's slave and stood aside in bewilderment at the chaos. Jamaica grabbed bags of oats and corn and slung them over the mules' necks. Quamana gathered harnesses and tackle.

Bo hobbled into the stable on his crutches. Wordlessly, he took a set of reins from Quamana and slid the harness over a horse's head. Together they readied every horse and mule in the stables.

Quamana said to Jamaica, "Ready?" He cupped his hands for her foot and lifted her onto a broad-backed gray mare.

He turned to Bo and clapped a hand on his shoulder. Bo gripped Quamana's arm. Though he had to stay behind, they had become brothers, in slavery, and now in freedom.

Then Quamana took the reins of a stallion and led the string of animals out into the rain.

By now, there were dozens of black men and women around the periphery of the house staring at the wild looting, wide-eyed and frightened. Serafina stood among them, a shawl draped over her head and shoulders, the rain dripping off her nose.

"Jamaica!" Serafina called. "What you doing? You gone get youself killed."

"Master already done that, Serafina," she called down from her horse. "You get on back out of the rain. Then you wait. We gone burn this road from here to New Orleans, then we come back and make you a free woman."

"Quamana, you gone get her killed!"

Jamaica had already made her choice. Quamana spurred his horse on, in his hand the reins of a buckskin for Kook.

Though his blood was up, the excitement coursing through his nerves, Quamana marshaled the rebels into an ordered formation and enforced their wait for Charles's forces to reach them. They would march down river together, all the way to New Orleans.

Kook dashed through the rain, a slicker over his broad shoulders, and took the buckskin's reins.

"You didn't fire the house?" Quamana asked.

"Too many damned fools won't get out of the man's wardrobe. It'll wait."

To one side, the river rushed by, swollen and swift after days of relentless rain. On the other side of the road, plantation homes, quarters, fields, orchards. And beyond those, the trackless swamp and flooded forests. This was a tactical problem, being confined to this twenty-foot ribbon of access to New Orleans. In Africa, they would use the terrain to hide, to surprise, to ambush. Here, their whereabouts would be no secret: the whites would know exactly where to find them.

Their strength would be in their numbers. In this parish, and the next and the next, there were many more slaves than whites, and they fought for their lives.

The sun lightened the gray skies in spite of the rain clouds. Louder and louder, the drums from upriver approached, pounding the march, urging on young men drunk with freedom and power and possibility. Behind them, smoke plumes from burning mansions fought their way upward through the rain. The rebels still turning over Brown's house poured out the front door and rushed to fall in with their fellows. The slaves who chose the familiar, who were too cautious to reach for such a wild dream, melted back into the plantation, away from the terrible danger and recklessness.

Charles approached in a din of drums and chanting, flags waving behind him, his raucous men in odd pairings of feathered militia caps and canvas pants tied with a rope at the waist. Quamana watched the architect of their liberation astride his undistinguished aging mount. The nag leant him an air of modesty, but the man himself seemed ten feet tall, radiating power and certainty. This man, Charles Deslondes, would lead them into a new country.

Kook, towering over his men on the bare back of the buckskin, raised his blade on high and let loose a war cry to pierce the rain and drums and scores of yelling voices. Charles, who never smiled, raised his arm in answer, his face split by a grin as maniacal as Kook's.

Chapter Twenty-One

Charles fought the urge to race forward as they neared Trépagnier's plantation—he wanted the man dead, if no other white in all the world were to die this day, let it be François Trépagnier—but he restrained his horse so as not to leave his army behind, those young men full of wild energy, nearly crazed with sudden power. They stayed in formation behind their leaders. Within their ranks, however, their movements were erratic and frenzied. They bounced on the balls of their feet as they marched, they pumped their arms, waving flags and weapons overhead, all the while they shouted and chanted, "On to New Orleans," and sometimes, from the more blood-thirsty ranks, "Death to the whites!"

By now, surprise was not possible. The drums and word-of-mouth had spread the news well ahead of them. Trépagnier had women in his household to protect. He likely had taken them into the back country to hide. Another day, Charles promised himself. Trépagnier could not hide forever. He would find him in the swamp, or cowering in New Orleans, and Charles would yield to this one last indulgence: he would execute this man.

Through the downpour rose the misty white columns of the Trépagnier mansion. Seconds later, a puff of smoke appeared on the second floor gallery, a second puff, and then the boom of the planter's shotgun traveled through the rain. Trépagnier was still here, and he was going to fight! Charles surged forward, but a wild figure ran into the road, arms waving. His horse reared up and Charles pulled the reins hard to the side to keep from running her over.

"Charles!" Rain streaming over her face, Annique clawed at his leg before he could dismount. "Charles!"

He slid off his horse and dug his fingers into her arms. "You could have been killed rushing under a horse like that!"

"They said it was you. They said you was the one leading them. Charles, they gone kill you, you do this." Her hands grasped the sodden militia uniform trying to hold him to her.

Charles glanced again at the gallery engulfed in musket smoke. Quamana and his troops had already rushed the house and were on the lower gallery breaking up the relatively dry wood of the gallery's furniture to set fires against the walls. Kook dashed for the back of the mansion.

The rebels, like a river of angry young men, flowed around him and Annique.

"Charles! Please!"

Charles pulled her close to his side and pushed through the thronging rebels to the shelter of an overhanging live oak. "Annique, go back," he shouted over the storm. "Stay in the cabin. I don't want you in this."

"Charles, please. They'll kill you, you know it. It's not too late. We'll go to Mr. Andry. We'll tell him you tried to stop it, you tried to keep him safe."

"Andry's dead. There is no going back." He should have prepared her for this, he could see that now. He should have explained. "Annique, I don't want to go back. This is for us. For all of us. We're going to be free."

Her face crumpled. "I don't want to be free if it mean you dead. I don't want to live if you dead."

He cupped her face in his hands, insisting she look at him. "Annique. I won't live a slave's life. My son won't live a slave's life. You, Annique, you and me and our children, we'll be free after this day."

She collapsed against him, sobbing. He held on to her and wished he could make her feel what he felt. His whole life had led to this day, to this wild elation coursing through his veins, a mad joy pushing him on. They made history here on this road!

He spoke into her ear so she would hear him over the rain. "We will have justice, Annique, and we will have our freedom. And then we will raise our family. Our children will be free."

He took her arms from around his neck. "Look at me, Annique. I love you. You promised to remember that."

She only nodded, sobs shaking her body.

"I will do this. And I will come back for you." He held her face in his hands and kissed her, certainty and conviction and promise in his touch. He hoped she could believe him, for he believed it now. He would come back for her. They would have a future together.

Holding her tight under his arm, he ran with her into the lashing rain to the slaves who stood aside, watching the master's cloud of gun smoke billow from under the gallery eaves as mad men climbed the stairs and burst through windows. He found Annique's auntie in the crowd. "Take her back," he said. "She's too cold. Please, get her to the cabin, stay with her."

Auntie held her arms open for Annique and pulled her away from the noise of breaking glass and gunfire and shouting. Frightened and crying, Annique reached for him, but the old woman held her fast.

"I'll come for you. Go home," he insisted.

He watched her stagger, her gaze on him as her aunt tugged her through the storm. When he was sure she was safe, he raced through the rain, mud sucking at his boots, and climbed the back stairs three at a time. Tearing through the house, he pulled the dagger from his belt and hoped he wasn't too late.

Trépagnier's shotgun fell silent. A shriek rose over the sound of the rain, and primitive cries of triumph pierced the sodden air.

Charles rushed onto the gallery to see Kook raise his hatchet for another killing blow, to see the slave Gustave stabbing his master over and over and over. Blood splattered the floor, the wall, their faces and bodies.

Even in his hatred for Trépagnier, Charles had not imagined such fury. He looked away, sickened at the smell of blood and guts and animal lust.

From below the gallery, he heard the whoosh and crackle of fire. Quamana would be spilling lamp oil over the floors beneath them.

"Kook!" Charles called. "The place is going up. We have to get out."

Kook's hatchet cracked into the dead man's bones and he raised it for yet another blow. "Kook!" Charles grabbed his arm and shoved him away from the corpse. The crazed look on Kook's face set him back, and for a moment he feared Kook would raise the hatchet against him. But the man was a soldier. He backed away and wiped a hand across his mouth. He stared at the bloody mess on the gallery floor, at the slave in a dog's collar grunting with every stab of his knife into the master's pulped body.

Smoke rose through the gallery floor and shouts filled the air. The deranged look in Kook's eyes dimmed as he came to himself. He stepped behind the dog boy and grabbed the collar. "Enough," he said. He hauled the boy up and pushed him into the house. Charles led them to the back stairs as smoke billowed up through the chimneys and floorboards.

Mud sucked the shoes off their feet. Horses and mules faltered in the mire. Some of the rebels chanced marching on top of the low levee, knowing a crumbling of the berm would send them tumbling into the swollen river. Yet still they waved their makeshift flags and shouted their triumphs. Had they not sent the masters running into the swamps, had they not taken their horses and desecrated their houses?

Charles knew their euphoria. He felt it himself. But his head told him this had been too easy. There would yet be a price to pay. Brown and his neighbors had escaped, and by now every white man on both sides of the river knew they were on the march. If Chapin was right that there were too few soldiers to defend the city, much less the plantations, then the only resistance would come from the planters. And the planters would be fighting for their lives. But even with most of the slaves remaining on the sidelines, his rebels still greatly outnumbered the whites. He smiled grimly. In two days' time, they would take New Orleans and declare a new state, won by violence, yes, but founded on the same principles that fueled the French and Haitian revolutions: justice.

Through the obscuring rain, Charles did not see the threat at the Labranch plantation until he was so close to the row of armed men that a musket ball could shatter him before he heard the report.

The slave Pierre leveled his firearm at Charles's chest. Charles knew Pierre as he knew most of the top slaves along the river. While Charles only pretended to be his master's loyal servant, he had deemed that Pierre truly lived in loyal servitude. He had never approached him, never hinted to him that another life was possible. He'd been right not to trust him.

From under the brim of his dripping hat, Charles eyed the young men standing with Pierre, some with old hunting guns, some with knives and hoes. Young men who should be riding with him, not resisting him.

Pierre took aim, squinting against the rain pelting his face. "I ain't gone let you do yore mischief here," he shouted. "Get on, and I don't have to shoot none of you."

Charles's skin warmed where the shotgun pointed, where it would blow a hole through his chest if Pierre pulled that trigger.

"What's it to you, Pierre, if the master loses his sugar stockpile?"

Pierre's aim didn't waver.

"Look at us." Charles waved a hand at the mass of men behind him. "We'll take New Orleans in two days, and you and every slave on the river will be free."

From the corner of his eye, Charles saw Kook slide off his mount and disappear into the throng. Quamana, on his other side, did the same.

Charles's gaze bore into each of the young men lined up with Pierre. "You'll have your freedom. Every one of you!"

The young men eyed the throng of rebels edging around Charles like an army of unstoppable ants, pouring into the lanes of the plantation. They snuck glances at Pierre, and at each other.

He nearly had them. "You want freedom? Take it!" Charles shouted.

Three of the defenders turned on their heels and ran into the mass of rebels bound for New Orleans and glory. The others, wavering now, looked from Charles to Pierre, but Pierre remained steadfast, his aim fixed on Charles's chest.

Charles saw Kook and Quamana gliding like jungle cats to come at Pierre from behind. He'd be glad when that damned musket wasn't pointed at his heart.

As the two Africans circled around soundlessly, Charles gave his ultimatum. "The rest of you," Charles said, no hint of conciliation in his voice, "join us, or we'll kill you where you stand."

The line broke, running into the army that flowed into the plantation to get at their plunder. Pierre swerved his aim and fired at the defectors, the boom echoing off the walls of the mansion behind him, the smoke quickly drowned in the downpour.

At that moment Quamana pounced, grabbing the shotgun. Kook threw Pierre to the ground. Charles touched his chest where Pierre's gun would have blown him open.

Charles dismounted and stood over Pierre lying in the mud, Kook's foot on his chest. "Why, Pierre?"

"It ain't right, what you do."

"But it's right to make a man a slave?"

"It ain't right," Pierre repeated. He hardened his jaw and turned his head away.

"Shoot him," Kook said.

Charles stared at the man in the mud who chose his master over his own freedom. Killing him would make a striking example to the other slaves of what happens to men who stand in their way. But Pierre was one of them. Even if he didn't thirst for freedom, he was a black man enslaved by white men. Charles didn't want to begin the new world by turning on each other.

Kook stepped close and raised his hatchet.

"No," Charles said.

Kook glared at him, fire in his eye. Charles met his defiance with a steady gaze.

"That's not how we do things," Charles said.

"You think we're going to do this without shedding blood?" Kook hissed. "Is that what you think? It's going to be all high-sounding talk of freedom, of justice, and no one gone get hurt?"

"Two white men are dead, and by now, Andry, too. And I'm not sorry. But this isn't about the killing. You've spilled enough blood, Kook. Take Pierre to a shed somewhere and lock him up."

Kook's anger smoldered between them. Rain streamed over the raised scars on his face, reminding Charles of the ferocity it had taken to earn those marks. All along, he had underestimated the man whose easy manner and smiling face seemed to belie the scars. He braced himself for an attack, keenly aware Kook's weapon was in his hand while his own was in his belt.

Quamana touched Kook's arm. Kook turned away.

Charles breathed out in relief.

They marched on, the Labranch plantation in flames behind them. No sign yet of the whites coming to fight for their homes and livelihoods, but they would. Charles called Mathurin to ride at the front of the army while he and Kook and Quamana sheltered in a mansion abandoned by whites and slaves alike. Charles didn't bother to wipe his muddy boots before he walked into the fine parlor. Embers in the grate still smoldered, and he stoked and fed them, then warmed his hands over the fire.

Quamana picked up a decanter and held it to the firelight, admiring the play of light off the crystal facets. He unstoppered it and sniffed the bourbon, curious and tempted.

"You drink that, you'll be muddle-headed," Charles said.

"You ever had any?"

"Bourbon? No. But I smelled it on Gilbert Andry often enough to know I don't want any."

"Gilbert's the one *you* killed," Kook said.

Charles looked at him. This hot-headed young man taunted him that he was as blood-thirsty as he was? Yes, he had wanted to kill Trépagnier himself, and he had killed Gilbert Andry. But one blow had satisfied him whereas Kook had mutilated François Trépagnier in a frenzy of bloody excess. Charles would never forget that sight, nor the smell.

Quietly, Quamana said, "We are not enemies here."

Kook gave a decisive nod and sat on the horsehair sofa, rainwater puddling at his feet.

"I'm going to look for food," Charles said. He walked into the dining room and into the butler's pantry where he found a bowl of sweet potatoes and a platter of ham. He took them back to the fire where the three of them ate ravenously.

The ham reduced to bone, Quamana said, "The men are getting tired."

"We'll stop before it gets dark," Charles said. "Give the men a chance to find someplace out of the rain, get something to eat."

Charles eyed a fine lace doily, decided the niceties of lace and napkins had no place in the world he was creating, and wiped his greasy hands on it. "They've done well. Burned a few homes, burned the sugar sheds. No killings I know of." He nodded at Kook. "Except ours. I salute you, and all the other captains. This is a true army, not a band of ruffians," Charles said with sincere pride.

"We are not savages," Quamana said. "But we have yet to face our enemy. They're out there waiting for us."

"We'll send scouts ahead."

Kook swallowed the nub end of a sweet potato, skin and all. "It is done. I sent four men out two hours ago."

"If they try to warn us using the drums," Quamana said, "we'll never hear them over our own din."

"That's why I sent four. They'll relay what they learn back to us."

"Good." From his pocket Charles took a sketch of the river road marked with the major plantations. He pushed the decanter on its silver tray aside and laid it flat on the table.

"We're here. Here's New Orleans. There are dozens of planters between here and the city, and you have to figure some of those who escaped us upriver have crossed over and made it to New Orleans by now. They'll be gathering with whatever militia Governor Claiborn can send to help them."

"How many are we now?" Quamana asked.

"I lost count. Over three hundred I think. And the maroons will be with us soon, maybe join up here," Charles said, pointing to his map.

They were quiet as they realized what that meant. Hundreds of them, against a few dozen frightened planters run out of their homes.

Charles stared at the map. There were miles of mud and wet and hazard between them and New Orleans, but on this paper, only inches between them and victory. Tomorrow they would reach the city. Tomorrow they would take the city.

"We can do this," Charles said, a note of awe in his voice.

"We will do this," Kook answered.

Chapter Twenty-Two

Soaked and chilled to the bone, the army slogged on down the river road, collecting rebels as they marched. They passed porticoes they had whitewashed, gardens they had tended, trees they had trimmed into cones and spirals. They had trained the rose vines over lattices and arbors, they had laid the wandering paths through flower gardens. All for someone else to enjoy on a summer evening. But no more. Beaten down by the rain, these flowers and gardens would bloom again, and they would belong to them, the people who dared to take what was due them.

Quamana pushed on, Jamaica at his side. She never faltered, never wearied. She would bear fine sons yet, if she lived. He hoped they would be his sons. But they had not yet earned their future.

Between two mansions a modest frame house nestled under live oaks. Out front, a wooden sign swung in the wind. It was painted with letters and with snakes twined around a staff. He'd seen the same design on the red-haired woman's bag when she came to tend to Bo's foot. Then this was the doctor's house. A faint plume of blue smoke rose from the chimney. Men from Mathurin's band were close behind him. The doctor was not liked among the slaves. They would not treat him or his house kindly.

"Wait here," he said to Jamaica. He spurred his horse toward the house and dismounted. He pushed through the door and found the red-haired woman sitting calmly in a rocking chair before a fire.

She stared at him, no fear in her face.

"Why didn't you run?"

"Your arm has healed well?" she said.

Quamana strode through the three rooms. "The doctor has gone. Why didn't you go with him?"

"I've done nothing to your people. Why should I run?"

"Because you're white. Because they will burn this house."

Resolute, Miss Evie stood up and shook her skirts out. "I shall not allow it." She marched to the front porch and planted herself with her arms crossed.

Quamana followed her, wondering if she were mad. The rebels were swarming across the yard now. Until now, they'd hardly encountered a white person. They'd all fled. And here was a defenseless white woman, kin of the doctor who sometimes caused more hurt than healing. They cried out as they ran, knives and sabers held high.

Quamana stepped behind her, two feet of towering black African looming over her shoulders.

His presence did not stop them. They surged around him and the woman and swept into the house. But they didn't touch Miss Evie.

Behind him, he heard them breaking furniture to make kindling. He grabbed the woman by her arm and hauled her into the rain. She wore only a knitted shawl and the rain soaked her through in moments. He tugged her through the yard and around to the back. Through the neighboring plantation's orchard, past its stables and barns, and into the slave quarters. Her feet hardly touched the muddy ground he pulled her along so quickly. By the time they reached the first cabin, her fiery hair was dark and straggled.

He tugged her up the stairs onto the porch and without knocking opened the cabin door. Inside were three women, two men, and half a dozen children huddled around the fire. One of the men, one of the women, and a boy child jumped to their feet. The boy rushed Quamana to defend his family, no matter that he might be ten years old and not even half Quamana's size. Quamana caught the boy and enveloped him in tight arms. The boy struggled.

Miss Evie stepped forward. "This very large man means you no harm. I believe he only wants to ask you if you will shelter me."

"Josiah, you stop," the woman said. "Miss Evie, you welcome to stay with us. I hope you be safe here."

Quamana set the boy down and he ran to his mama.

"Will we be safe here?" Miss Evie asked him.

"These people," he said, nodding toward the slaves huddled together, "are our people. We fight to free them, too."

"As I thought." As if she were in a fine gown at a soiree instead of in a slave cabin with wet hair and muddied gown, she held out her hand. "You may have saved my life. Thank you."

This white woman meant for him to take her hand? A hand no bigger than a child's, white, and freckled. Quamana very gently engulfed her hand with his own. She pumped his arm once, and then let go.

He glanced at the slaves. He nodded to the red-haired woman and turned to leave.

She held the door as he passed through it.

"God go with you," she murmured, and he ran through the storm to rejoin the rebels.

Above the Destrehan plantation, the long-awaited maroons emerged from the woods and slipped through orchards and fields. Charles sent Kook to welcome Big Tom, the two of them embracing.

Charles knew now that Kook had dared the storm to get his wife and children to the maroons. Not many months ago, Charles would have killed him for it. He had risked the rebellion itself if their flight had been discovered. But it had not been discovered.

The rebels, now reinforced by dozens of maroons, marched on in adrenaline-fueled exultation, buoyed by the enormity of what they had accomplished so far. But Charles watched for signs of flagging, and as another line of black clouds roiled toward them, he called a halt. They needed to make camp before dark, to get warm, to rest. They had eaten what they found as they passed through the various plantations like a horde of locusts, but they needed something hot in their bellies to get through the cold night to come.

The men spread out over the plantation. The lucky ones filled the barns and sheds or crowded into the quarters, welcomed or not. Some commandeered the mansion itself and lay themselves on wool carpets and brocade sofas. Some dared to lie in the white family's beds and marveled at the comfort of a feather mattress and linen sheets.

Outside, the rebels dug trenches to drain a patch of ground and rigged shelter out of tarps and stacks of firewood. Charles walked through the camps, breathing in the smell of hundreds of jubilant men, drunk on possibility and hope. Some roasted chickens over their fires, some spitted haunches of fresh-killed pork. He spoke to the men as he passed by, congratulating them on their first day of freedom, laughing with them in their high spirits. But his own elation had waned with the daylight. They had been lucky. There had been no real resistance, not yet. But there would be.

Chilled to the bone in his sodden boots and jacket, he returned to the overseer's cabin he had made his headquarters. Kook and Quamana and Mathurin had the fire burning hot and a pot of chicory brewing. He breathed in the heady aroma and started peeling off his wet clothes.

Half naked, their clothes spread out to dry, the four of them ate what they found in the larder. Charles only picked at the peas and ham. All he wanted was a warm dry bed, to close his eyes for just a few minutes, but tomorrow they would face the enemy. They had to be ready. Some of the planters might cower in the swamp, but others would be gathering forces and searching for the men who'd rousted them from their homes, who'd humiliated them. They'd be out for blood.

The door burst open and a man blew into the cabin with the wind and the rain.

Charles leapt to his feet, reaching for his hatchet.

Kook held a hand up. "That's Remo. He's one of mine."

Rain poured off the boy's bare head, his shoulders, his boots. He looked ready to drop, but Kook grabbed him, kicked the door shut, and led him to the fire.

"Get him a cup of that chicory," Kook said. He peeled the clothes off his scout and tossed them down in front of the fire. Now he was undressed, Charles saw he was no more than fourteen or fifteen. He shivered so violently his teeth chattered and his knees knocked together. Kook grabbed a quilt off the overseer's bed and wrapped it around the boy's shoulders.

"They's coming," the boy stuttered.

"Where?" Kook demanded.

"Let him have the chicory," Mathurin said. "We can wait two minutes."

Kook turned on him with a snarl. "Two minutes? What if they're two minutes from here?"

Charles had misjudged these two Africans all along. Quamana had seemed the greater menace, his rage simmering just below the surface. But now the time had come, Quamana had the cooler head, and Kook was a terrible, destructive force.

"No. No, they're not," Remo stammered. "Down river, maybe ten miles."

"Who are they?"

"Man riding in front had stars on his collar." Remo looked at Kook and then at Quamana. "And Master Brown, he ride beside him."

Kook cursed and paced the room.

"How many?" Charles asked.

He held out his hands and flashed ten at them, and again and again. Maybe a hundred, then. "They was in uniforms, and they was all on horses."

Their rebels were tired. They were poorly armed and inexperienced. Charles couldn't imagine his men had kept their powder dry. Many were still without mounts. But the enemy were mounted, well-armed, and had practiced military men with them. Claiborn had kept back some militia after all.

"We need to choose the time and place to fight," Charles said. "Not them."

Quamana nodded toward Kook. "In our home, we often faced an army better armed than ours. We know what to do."

They made their plans, pulled on their damp clothes, and stepped back into the downpour. It had been raining steadily for four days. The mud sucked at them, wearying them, but the same mud sucked at the whites coming after them, the same rain pelted and chilled them.

The organization Charles had instilled in his rebels paid off now. Each lieutenant gathered his men and in spite of darkness, rain, mud, and cold, they accomplished the tasks set for them.

At midnight, Charles sent his army back up the river road in orderly retreat. Tomorrow, they would choose their ground, they would be ready, and they would face the better-armed but out-numbered whites. They would grind them down, they would run them over, and then they'd push on to New Orleans. By now, Chapin would have taken the armory and secured the government buildings around the Place d'Armes, and with any luck, he'd have the governor himself in chains.

Charles stayed behind. He rode down the road and then turned back to approach the encampment and see it as the whites would. Fires glimmered through the brush, then as he turned the curve of the road, he clearly saw the blazes, some small, some large. Shelters with their backs to the wind rose darkly beside the fires. Around the perimeter, they'd built a make-shift picket fence with huddled straw mounds that Charles hoped would look like sleeping sentinels.

He wished he could stay to see the white general ready his men in the darkness. Their horses would be restless, sensing the excitement of their riders. The men would be drenched, but determined and thirsty for the blood of ungrateful slaves who'd turned them from their homes. They'd prime their weapons, unsheathe their blades, and exchange manic grins in the dark wet night. The general would give the signal. They'd charge headlong, galloping into the rebel camp, sabers raised to stab and slash, guns firing – at nothing.

Charles rejoined his army. The men were quiet, tired, wet and cold. They marched miles and miles in the murky dark over the same ground they'd taken the day before. Morning came and they passed houses they'd sacked, doors left open banging in the wind. Where they'd torched a mansion, they smelled the smoky embers.

Charles's bones ached and in his fatigue his head bent without his willing it. In a fog of dream and memory, he leaves his muddy boots and dripping poncho on Annique's porch. He eases into the cabin, builds up the fire, and warms himself while she sleeps, the cat curled up at her hip. Firelight reveals the fine veins of her eyelids and the gentle curve of her cheek. He bends to kiss her. She smiles, his Annique, and lifts her arms to welcome him home.

"Charles!"

Mathurin shoved at his shoulder.

"You sleeping in the saddle? I thought you were going to slide right off your horse."

"I'm fine," he said, wiping the rain from his forehead. "Whose place is that ahead?"

"We're nearly back to Bernoudy's. How far you mean to go?"

The rain was only spitting at them now. Charles looked west hoping he'd see a hint of blue sky, but there were more clouds scudding their way. "We'll stop at Bernoudy's. Pass the word. And send Kook to me."

Kook brought another young scout with him and the three of them stood off the road while the rebels filed past. "Tell him what you saw last night."

"Yessir. I seen them whites rush in like they could see in the dark," the boy said. "They was waving torches and shooting off they guns, shouting and shrieking like all they racket would scare us to death." The boy grinned at Kook. "It was a sight, Kook. You should a seen it."

"Go on," Charles said.

"They was mad we wasn't there. They tore down all them tarps and such we set up. They rode around looking in the sheds seeing if any of us were fool enough to be hiding out. But they didn't find me. I was in a big old magnolia tree, way up high. They couldn't see me, and I didn't get but half soaked under them big leaves."

"Where are they now?"

"They probably still there. They laid up to rest, just like we did, only they don't got so many as us. They mostly squeezed into the big house and the barns up out of the rain. They was all asleep when I slipped off."

"You did a man's work last night. Go on and join your friends," Kook said, nodding toward the army marching past them. "We'll stop soon and you can find something to eat."

Kook and Charles stood watching the men flow by. Fire and ice, Charles thought. That's what some might think of the two of them, Kook in his ferocity, Charles with his methodical planning. But at this moment, Charles felt they were brothers, close as men born from the same sac in their mother's belly, united now in common purpose.

Charles looked at his brother in arms. Kook and Quamana had planned a brilliant ruse, and it had worked. "Would your army back in Africa have fallen for that trick last night?"

Kook's smile spread into a grin.

Charles laughed. "That's what I thought."

A surge of energy and renewed confidence warmed his blood. They'd outsmarted the best Governor Claiborn had to offer.

He'd let his rebels rest a few hours, then they'd turn downriver again and meet this force from New Orleans, a force who'd fallen for an old trick. They could be beaten, this ragged mix of planters and soldiers. By nightfall, New Orleans.

He threaded through his men as they slogged through the mud, hardly less elated this morning than they had been the day before. They waved their flags, they sang and they chanted. Kook's scouts had spread the word. They knew they'd bested the whites last night. They knew they were on the glory road to freedom.

Ducking under a waving flag, Charles stepped up onto the levee to have a look at the river. The Mighty Mississippi they called her. Muddy gray water swirled in eddies near the shore. Out in the current, a tree big as a house rushed by. The river didn't care whether it was whites or blacks who shipped their goods on her back, but soon it would be blacks harvesting their own crops and sending them down to New Orleans. Blacks steering pirogues like that one crossing the river to visit kinfolks or trade their crafts.

Charles peered at the pirogue maybe a thousand yards upstream as it crossed from the opposite bank. The boat was overloaded, and they chose to hazard the river in this weather, with this swollen current?

The hair prickled on the back of his neck. Those were musket barrels sticking into the air above the shoulders of the men crowded into that pirogue. Another overloaded pirogue was pulling into shore, another and another.

They'd been flanked.

Charles pushed through his men to the front where his leaders rode. They must not be caught concentrated in this narrow band of the road, confined between river and woods.

"Mathurin! Kenner!" He knew this stretch of road, knew the Bernoudy plantation and the two that abutted it. "We'll make our stand there," he pointed.

His heart thrummed in his chest, his blood rushed through his veins. This was it. What he'd wanted all his life, what he had schemed and plotted for, patiently, relentlessly. To the beat of a hundred drums, the lieutenants rushed to arrange their men across a plowed field.

Charles didn't know how many planters had crossed the river in their pirogues, but even a dozen, or three dozen pirogues could not carry enough men to stop them. He need only defeat them before the whites downriver caught up to them.

He watched his officers carry out his orders, spreading the rebels out in ranks along the width of a plowed field. The men jostled and shouted and grinned, eager for the battle to come. They felt it, too, this quickening joy and keen elation. As he passed their ranks, Mathurin at his side, his men roared their readiness and shook their machetes, pikes, and sabers over their heads. They could have stayed behind, cowering in the swamp or hiding in the quarters, but they had chosen to risk everything for this chance. These men were the future. These men would build a new country.

As the drums resounded and the men roared, Charles felt his heart swell into his throat. He could scarcely breathe for the pride he felt in every man on that field. And in that moment, he felt blessed with a strangely peaceful exaltation.

Kook dashed up and pulled his horse to a hard halt. "They're coming."

"We're ready," Charles said.

Kook stared hard at Charles as he steadied his dancing horse. "Manuel Andry leads them."

For a moment, Charles could not take it in. "Andry?"

Kook's eyes accused him. "You let him go, didn't you? And he crossed the river and raised an army."

A single thread of ice ran through Charles's gut. Kook was right. He'd made a mistake. Men would die today, some of them his own, because he had not let Cable chase down Manuel Andry.

"Look around you," Mathurin said. "We are hundreds. We will send them back to the river, or to their graves."

Kook didn't bother to answer. He turned his horse and trotted to his own men.

On foot, Quamana dashed through the rain. This was all wrong. The men knew nothing about white-man's warfare, nothing about how to handle themselves in this kind of fight. They were not even prepared for the noise that was about to break over them, not just the drums but hundreds of voices raised in battle cry, horses' hooves thundering toward them, guns firing. They had no idea how such a din disoriented and confused. They had no notion of the kind of courage it took to face a gun or a saber when you had a choice—stay and fight or run for your life.

"Charles!" he yelled. "Move them back. Into the woods. You can't line these boys up like soldiers."

Charles looked down at him from atop his horse, the rain spilling off the brim of his hat. "What are you talking about?"

"If you stand here and wait for the whites to come at us, we will fail. We don't have that kind of training, we don't have the experience for that kind of battle. Take us into the woods. We can spread out, save the main force of our army while a squad circles around and comes at them unawares. We don't have to defeat every white to win this battle. We just have to pick off a few of them and the rest will run."

Charles looked at his army, shuffling into ranks, staring into the rain where they expected the enemy to appear. He saw Kook correcting a man's grip on his pike, Harry Kenner showing another how to hold a saber.

"Charles! We talked about this. We are not an army," he slung his arm toward the rebels massing behind him. "Not like this. Our strength —"

"They have guns. We have guns," Charles shouted over the drums. "We outnumber — "

"How many of us ever fired a gun before, even know how to get a musket primed and loaded? All our guns will do is make noise and smoke, the ones that manage to go off in this rain. Call a retreat. We'll take them later when — "

A barrage of musket fire roared through the sodden air. They could barely see the advancing whites through the downpour, but second by second they emerged slogging through the mud, the second wave of guns going off. A man standing behind Quamana threw his hands into the air, a fountain of blood spraying from his neck.

Charles whirled his horse around, raised his saber and yelled, "Fire!"

"Fool!" Quamana cried. "They're too far. Hold your fire! Hold fire!"

No one heard him over the roar of the enemy's musketry, the drums, the war cries. All of the rebels armed with firearms made up the front row, they'd known enough to do that, but they all fired at once, those that had dry powder and a loaded gun.

Their shots went wild, into the ground, into the air. They'd never aimed a weapon, never gauged the wind. They fumbled to reload, struggled to remember the steps in order.

Kook ran from man to man, hurrying him, helping him reload, all the while shouting to the others "Pan, cartridge, prime, load, ram. Pan, cartridge, prime, load, ram..."

Remo plucked from the mud the musket of the man whose neck had erupted in a spray of arterial blood. With a wild glint in his eye and a grin on his face, he offered it to Quamana. Over the roar of the drums and gunfire, Quamana yelled "Down!" and bore hard on Remo's shoulder. Too late. A musket ball pierced the boy's head, just above the ear. Remo hardly jerked, but the gleam in his eye died and slowly his knees folded and he collapsed into the mud, the musket still in his hands.

Quamana knelt, his hand still on Remo's shoulder. He shook himself. He had no time for this. He yanked the musket from under the boy and slicked the mud off the trigger.

He peered down the barrel, chose his man, and fired. He missed. He rushed into the rhythm of pan, cartridge, prime, load, ram all the while the white line steadily advanced. They were twenty yards closer now. He wouldn't miss next time.

He aimed, he fired. A plume of mud shot up near his target's foot. Again. Pan, cartridge, prime, load, ram. All around him the rebels rushed through the same frantic ritual, firing at will, missing, missing, and missing again.

Let them get close enough we can charge them, Quamana prayed. We can take them if we get in with our blades, if we can hold out another minute.

Charles fought with his men from Andry's plantation, Justice and Cable, Jupiter, Henry, and Marshal. He had shown them how to ready a musket for loading and firing, but it had been mere pantomime. With cold wet fingers, they bungled and fumbled trying to reload. He raised his ancient shotgun and fired. The wind was against them, the rain...Quamana was right. They were not prepared for this kind of warfare. He had blundered. Again.

Beside him, Caleb clutched at his gut, blood pouring over his hands.

"Pan, cartridge, prime..." he chanted to the men struggling with their weapons. He reloaded, aimed, fired. "Pan, cartridge, prime..."

Quamana had lost sight of Jamaica, but he couldn't stop to find her. He aimed once more and fired his last ball. He couldn't see a single fallen white through the gray curtain of rain, but men on either side of him bled into the muddy ground. The fire from his own rank grew thin and scattered. They were running out of ammunition and dry powder. But the planters were not. They continued to fire relentlessly into the ranks, their balls opening chests and heads and bellies.

Quamana threw his useless gun into the mud and drew the saber at his waist. His men crowded around him, waiting for his signal to charge in with their plundered pikes and machetes and swords.

His blood chilled at a horse's terrified shriek, its eyes rolling as blood spurted from its neck. It reared, it collapsed, and still it screamed. The rebel nearest him broke into sobs, his whole body trembling. Quamana had seen brave men pushed over into panic by just one more horror, and had then seen that man's fear spreading in waves to other men as if it were a rolling, rushing tide.

They couldn't wait any longer.

"Death to the whites!" he screamed and rushed across the killing ground, saber raised. His rebels screeched in full battle cry, sprinting to reach the planters' line before they were shot down.

One man, death marching mercilessly toward him, overwhelmed by noise and terror, threw his weapon to the ground and sprinted back through the ranks, running away from the ceaseless hail of musket balls.

Another, and then another followed. And the wave of panic rushed through the rebel army. Desperate for the safety of the woods, the men ran.

Charles fired his last shot and threw down his gun. With his hatchet in one hand, a knife clutched in the other, he rushed to join Quamana's charge, his battle scream drowned out by the roar of drums and muskets.

His body knew what it needed to do, charge across the fifty yards between him and the enemy, but his mind – somehow his mind remained above it all, watching himself and all his hopes and plans struggle to endure. They could surely, they in their hundreds, defeat these few score of men. And yet. What if they could not succeed? He knew some of the men behind him had run, maybe most of them; he knew the rebels rushing across this field with him were dying, their blood running thinly into the rain and the soil. The next ball might be for him. He might die, here, now.

He surged through the rain, fighting the mud that sucked at his boots, and bared his teeth as he rushed on, hatchet raised to smash the first white man he reached. And then he saw Manuel

Andry kneeling as he took aim and fired the long-barreled gun at oncoming rebels.

Charles pivoted to head directly for the man who'd owned his body and his labor all these years, who had used his slaves as if they were born only for his pleasure. He would kill Manuel Andry before he died.

"Charles! Charles, stop!" Mathurin caught him by the arm and whirled him around. Charles raised his hatchet to fight him off, crazed with blood lust.

Justice, who had marched with them through all the cold wet miles, grabbed Charles's raised arm and shoved him back.

"Charles!" Mathurin shouted over the din. "Think, man. We need you. The men are in the woods, we can regroup. We can go on."

Charles shook his head, trying to clear the red haze from his mind.

"You die here, it's over. You understand?" Mathurin turned to Justice. "Get him out of here."

Justice, heavier and taller than Charles, seized his arm and ran him off the field, through the falling warriors, the whizzing musket balls, the screams and the blood.

A dozen strides past the tree line, Charles looked over his shoulder. Mathurin was not behind them. He jerked his arm free of Justice's grip. "Mathurin!"

"I'll get him. You keep going."

Charles shook his head and started back to the battlefield.

Justice grabbed him again. "You heard what he said. You no good to us if you dead."

Charles looked once more toward the horror of that field.

"It don't have to be over yet," Justice said.

Charles looked at the younger man, blood spattering his face and chest, someone else's blood. Justice stared at him steadily. "It don't have to be over yet," he repeated.

Charles nodded. He ran, the sounds of musketry popping through the woods. The drums had ceased, but his own heart gave him the cadence for his feet pounding over the soaked ground, leaping over fallen branches and tangling vines.

Quamana rushed on, twenty yards, ten. He sprang forward, his saber raised to slash down into the body of the hated white raising his gun for yet another shot. The end of the barrel erupted in a quick red flame and a puff of grey smoke. Before he felt the pain, before he realized he was shot, Quamana's face plowed into the muck.

Shot, he thought. Not dead. He pushed his hands into the muck to raise himself, to carry on until he was dead. Before he could get to his knees, two men tackled him. He twisted and grappled. A third man, and then a fourth fell on him, shoving his face down, suffocating him with mud, with the weight of four men pressing him into the mire. And still he fought. Until Manuel Andry raised the butt of his musket. Quamana's head seemed to explode with pain and flashing light, and then darkness.

Kook saw Quamana go down. Rage fueled his mad charge into the hail of musket balls. He would avenge Quamana with the last thrust of his blade, and he would die a man. His saber raised, screaming his death cry, he lunged forward -- but his saber flew from his hand and blood sprayed from the fingers blown off. As they had with Quamana, white men pounced on him and ground him into the earth.

Kook slung his bloodied hand into a white face, clawed at another with his good hand. He kicked. He bit, the man's blood filling his mouth. He contorted his back like a coil and sprung up into the mass of white men fighting to keep him down. But not even Kook could defeat six determined men. He saw the rifle butt coming and in the next instant, his body went limp. He was taken.

Charles ran deeper into the woods behind the plantation. Brush tore at his legs, puddles hid their depths. The rain renewed itself and his mind raced, calculating how many men had run, how many he could regroup. Some would run into the swamp, others would race through the back lanes to hide out in the quarters, to pretend they had never chanced everything to be free.

He tore on, looking for the trail back deep beyond the plantations to take him to the maroon encampment. They could set up a defense there if the whites dared follow. They could carry on the fight. Eventually, if not today, then soon, they'd finish this. His hands fisted and his jaw tightened. The new order was coming. The whites would fall.

Over the sounds of his heaving breath and the slapping of palmettos against his body, he heard a faint baying. He stumbled. *Oh please, God. Not the hounds.* Panic crept in, little tendrils at first, and then a strangling vine that choked the breath out of him. He couldn't get enough air, couldn't see through the rain and the gray film of terror. He staggered on, hope draining from his heart as the baying of the hounds sounded through the woods.

Wildly he looked for shelter, for safety from the tearing fangs of the dogs. But he had splashed into the low flooded area of towering cypress. No way to climb those smooth trunks, nowhere to hide.

He could make out the individual cries of the hounds now. They were closing in fast. He churned through the water, heedless of the dangers of the swamp. He heard the dogs splashing behind him. He heard their panting. His mind was simply gone. He knew only fear and the desperate push of his feet into the mud, out of the mud, and into the muck again, his arms wheeling as his knees pumped hard to clear of him of the water and the sucking bottom.

The lead hound snapped at his heel and missed, and then they were on him. Teeth tore into his legs, his feet, his arms. He curled into a ball and the terrible slashing and piercing went on and on.

A musket fired and Charles thought he was shot dead. The dogs left off. There was only the sound of their panting and whimpering, the sound of rain splattering through the treetops. Charles opened his eyes.

"Get up, nigger."

Slowly, reason returned. Charles saw the hounds, bouncing and whining with excitement. Half a dozen white men stood in a semicircle, their muskets pointed at him. He bled from dozens of wounds, but not from a musket ball.

He was caught. He was done for. For him, it was over.

Chapter Twenty-Three

Charles staggered, the hounds dancing all around him, nipping at him, half-crazed at the smell of his blood. Manuel Andry himself yanked at the rope tied around his hands. Others prodded him from behind, back through the woods, back to the bloody field where the remains of his army lay dead or captured.

The field was littered with the bodies of slaves slain by musket ball or saber thrust. Another pack of hounds and a score of white men with muskets primed and loaded encircled the slaves they'd captured. Unbelievably, after all they'd fought for, there were black men in the field who eagerly did the masters' bidding. Slaves to the depths of their souls.

Charles stumbled, dropping to his hands and knees. Andry jerked the rope, yanking his hands out from under him so that his chin and his chest slapped into the thick black muck. He lifted his head and saw what he'd known would happen. Across the field, standing over a dead rebel, a white man raised a well-honed machete and whacked it down, decapitating the body. Charles gagged, bitter bile rising in his throat.

"Give me a hand here," Andry called to a pair of slaves. They dragged him into the center of the field where his former soldiers could see him. Charles struggled to rise from the mud, blood still flowing from gashes and tears where the hounds had torn into him, but with the butt of his rifle, Andry pushed him back down and then shoved him over onto his back.

"You won't be getting up again," Andry said. He held out his hand and a slave gave him a heavy, iron-headed sledgehammer. He heaved the sledgehammer over his head and with all his strength pounded the iron head down onto Charles's thigh. He heard the bone snap as pain seared through his body. He was blind from shock when the blow came again, breaking his other thigh bone. His shriek came to him from a distance, as if some other poor creature wailed in agony.

Pain, cold, and shock possessed his body, and the part of his brain that felt every nerve, every sinew, muscle and bone aflame in torment opened his throat to scream his anguish into the air. His mind, though, separated itself from the being on the ground. His mind moved away so that Charles hovered over the scene, watching what they did to his body.

A great sadness overcame him. He'd tried so hard. All his life, he'd kept himself apart, had lived in loneliness with only a great dream to sustain him. And he had failed.

A blade raised over his body. Was this the last blow, or were they going to carve him up before they killed him? The blade came down. He did not die, but he heard the screams coming from his body and knew what they had done.

The sound of the screaming seemed muffled now and the pain moved even further from his mind. With that relief, a strange tranquility descended. He could see, now. What his life had been for. He had not been meant to create a new country. He had been meant only to try. After him, another man's destiny would be to try again, and then another, until some day, destiny would be fulfilled. They would be free. It was enough, what he had done.

The blade raised over his body again.

"Charles." The voice was sweet and soft. "Charles, come with me now." Annique held her hand out to him. "It's time to rest."

Charles took her hand and went with her to the warmth.

Quamana and Kook stood near the single window of the storeroom where the captives were jammed in so tight no man could lie down. Two days they'd been confined in this cold drafty room. The stink of fear and bodily waste, the stink of defeat, filled the air. Quamana no longer noticed the smell.

He'd watched Charles Deslondes die. He'd seen the heads on pikes lining the river road. His own head would soon be among them. Crows would come and fatten themselves on the flesh of brave men. Quamana did not flinch at the thought. When he'd been a small boy, his mother had sent him into the fields to wave a red cloth and shoo the crows away from the seeds she'd sown. They would rise in a great black cloud, squawking and complaining, and then he'd stand very still until they came back to feed. Then with great glee he'd wave the cloth and screech at them again, loving the whir of their wings as they fled from him. He liked crows.

Kook stood beside Quamana, staring out the window. The rain had stopped. Blue sky shone through the bare branches of the pecan trees. He was glad to see blue sky again. It was easier to imagine Rosie and Josh and little Lila happy under a blue sky.

The first night here in the storeroom had nearly undone him. It was dark. It stank. And bodies pressed against him on all sides so that he felt he would smother. In his fatigue, he thought he was deep in the hold of the slave ship again, enduring, suffering, and frightened. Then Quamana had gripped his arm and he knew he was safe. For now. Strange, he thought. On the ship, Kook had been the one who looked after Quamana, and now it was Quamana who steadied him.

The chains on the door rattled as the locks were opened. A man with a musket nodded at the two nearest captives, Justice and a man Quamana didn't know. "You two, come on out. Which ones are Kook and Quamana?"

The white guards took the four of them up the stairs of the big house into a grand room with a painted ceiling and a patterned carpet under foot. Half a dozen planters dressed in fine wool coats with white linen neck cloths sat behind a table.

The man in the middle spoke. "You boys have committed a grievous crime."

"Monsieur Destrehan, if I may," another planter interrupted. He dipped his quill into the ink pot. "Let me get their names written into the record."

Destrehan nodded.

One of the guards clad in homespun breeches and a cotton coat nudged the rebel next to Quamana with the end of his musket. "Give him your name."

"Nicolas."

"Who's your master?" asked the secretary with the pen.

"Mr. Bernoudy, sir."

"And you?" The man pointed his quill at Kook.

"Kook."

"And who is your master?"

"I have no master," Kook said.

The guard jabbed him with the muzzle of the musket, hard enough to take the breath out of him.

"We will return to you. Next?"

"Quamana."

"And your master is...?"

Quamana smiled and made no answer.

"These two both belong to James Brown," Manuel Andry said. "Get on with it."

"What is your name?" the secretary asked the last man.

"Justice. I don't belong to no man." For that act of defiance, the guard rapped the barrel of the musket against his ear. Justice reeled, but he kept his feet.

"He's one of mine," Andry said. "A new man. Charles himself brought him to my place." He sneered at Justice. "You a rebel from the first, that why Charles bought you with my money?"

Justice stared over Andry's head.

"Let's proceed," Destrehan said impatiently. "You boys know what we do to rebels. If you want to live, you will cooperate. We already know who your leaders are, and here are you two, Kook and Quamana, already condemned. Unless you help yourselves."

"Your fellow rebel, Cupidon," Andry said. "You know him. He will be allowed to live out his natural life. Because," he added with meaningful looks at each of them, "he cooperated. You, Nicolas. Who were your confederates who ran off into the woods? Give us names, and perhaps you can be spared as Cupidon is."

Quamana glanced at the man. He was of medium height, very dark skin. He was filthy with mud and waste, and he stank. The filth he could be forgiven, but Nicolas trembled with fear. His jaw quivered, and his eyes were huge and staring. Not a man, Quamana thought. He will tell them anything they want to hear.

"I knows some of them," Nicolas said, his voice quivering.

The secretary readied his pen. "Names? Owners, too, of course." The secretary turned to Andry. "The names are of little use without the owners' names as well. So many of them are named Suzanne or Pierre or Jean."

"Who were with you?" Andry said.

"There was Marcel, he come with me from Bernoudy's place. And so did Alvie."

"Very good. Who else?"

Quamana wanted to step away from the stink of Nicolas' cowardice, but he remained still. Let the man put himself back in servitude, if that's what he wanted.

"Barnaby, Claude, and Jacque, they was with us. And I seen that carpenter fellow, Paul, from Mr. Brown's place. And I knowed Charles Deslondes. He been to Bernoudy's before, and I seen him."

The secretary's quill scratched across the page, name after name. So many names, but none of it mattered. They were all dead men, Quamana thought. Nicolas might draw breath a little longer than he would, but inside, Nicolas had just killed himself.

"Justice. Who are the rebels you know by name?"

Justice did not respond.

"You hear me, boy? Name names or you die where you stand."

The guard moved in so his muzzle was inches from Justice's gut.

"Not on my carpet," Destrehan murmured.

"Who were your confederates? Save yourself, boy, while you can."

Andry tried next. "What of your own crimes? Which houses did you burn down?"

At Justice's stubborn silence, Andry lost his temper. "You will answer or I will shoot you down myself. Did you help Charles Deslondes kill my son?"

"He did it!" Nicolas burst out. "I know he did it. I heard him telling it, bragging how he kill Master Andry's boy."

Quamana had stood a day and a night in the crowded storeroom, this man Justice pushed up against him. He did not believe Justice had bragged about anything he had ever done. He cut his eyes toward Justice. He didn't seem to care whether Nicolas accused him falsely or not. Quamana looked next at Charles's old master. Andry's face burned bright red, his face a grimace of rage.

"I will have your head on a pike, boy. Think on that for the next hour until I have time for you. Take this—" Andry spluttered "—this thing out of here. You are not to kill him. I will do it myself."

The guard stuck his musket into Justice's back and marched him out. A moment later James Brown came in. "My apologies for being tardy, gentlemen." He paused, his eyes on Kook and Quamana. "So you have these two devils before you. Then I am in good time." He spread the tails of his frock coat and sat down.

Destrehan resumed the questioning. "Kook. You now have your opportunity to save yourself. Who were the slaves who joined you?"

The secretary poised his quill over the paper.

Kook looked at his judges with a mild expression. But he said nothing.

"You mean to tell me you had rather die this day than give up a few names?"

Quamana wondered, not caring much one way or the other, whether Kook would remain silent or would he choose to tell these white men sitting there in their pride to bugger themselves. It might be fun, for a few moments, if Kook chose to spit in their eyes.

But Kook chose silence.

Destrehan tried another tack. "You know Cupidon? Dagobert? Rebels, both of them. But they have redeemed themselves. Dagobert, for instance, accuses you, Kook, of setting fire to Mr. Laclaverie's house. Cupidon maintains it was you who axed our esteemed friend Monsieur Trépagnier to death. What say you to these charges?"

From the corner of his eye, Quamana saw the sudden relaxation of Kook's shoulders, the thrusting of one foot forward so that his hip was cocked, and Quamana's heart lightened. One more show of the affable slave before they died, and Quamana meant to enjoy it.

"I is happy to oblige you," Kook said, a goofy smile on his face. "I 'member Laclaverie's house burning down." He scratched his head like he was thinking. "It hard to 'member, so much been happening, but seem like I do that." He grinned like he suddenly remembered. "Yes, sir, that was me."

Brown snorted in disgust. "You cost me more than a prime racehorse, but I'll shoot you myself -- if nothing else, for your damned insolence."

"Hold on," the secretary said. "And the charge of killing Monsieur Trépagnier?"

"Oh, I remembers that just fine," Kook said. "That was me axed him so his blood spilt all over hisself. I got no trouble 'membering that."

The room was silent. No one moved. That was their friend whom Kook had hacked into a pulp. Quamana watched Andry who looked as though he might be sick.

"Get him out of here," Destrehan said, low.

Quamana spent another night in the storage shed though it was not so crowded now. Yesterday the whites had executed half a dozen. Today, it would be his turn, and Kook's.

They came for them after dawn. Hobbled, Quamana shuffled across the yard. He offered no resistance when the guards shoved him up against the post and bound him to it with rope wrapped around his chest. Kook was tied to the other post.

Quamana was glad to stand with Kook in their last moments. Glad the sun still shone. He closed his eyes and felt the warmth on his face. He'd had enough of rain.

He heard his executioners ready their weapons. Pan, cartridge, prime, load, ram...

"Ready..."

Quamana turned his head to Kook.

"Aim..."

Kook smiled at him.

"Fire."

Afterword

If the lion has no intention to attack,
it will not show its teeth before you.
-- Adage from the Asante Kingdom

A cast gold lion baring its teeth is on display in the Dallas Museum of Art. It is an artifact from the Asante people who lived in what is now Ghana. For them the lion represented the bravery of their chieftain, but since this gold lion has its teeth bared, it also perfectly illustrates the Asante adage. Despite it's rather impish look, this lion is ready to attack.

In 1811, the biggest slave revolt on American soil took place forty miles above New Orleans. Two of the ringleaders, Kook and Quamana, had been Asante warriors before they were captured and enslaved. Today the Akans are the dominant ethnic group in Ghana, and the Asante (also *Ahsanti*) kingdom was one of several among the Akans.

These two young men arrived in Louisiana in 1806. They were apparently about 15 and 20 years old, so they were still young men when the rebellion began 5 years later. Kook and Quamana were at that time toiling on the plantation belonging to James Brown on the Mississippi River.

Historians also have documentation about the rebel leader, Charles Deslondes. It is known he was a man of mixed blood working as a trusted slave driver on the plantation owned by Manuel Andry near what is now Laplace, Louisiana. It is also known that when the rebellion failed, his captors dealt him a horrific death.

Historians have evidence that this rebellion had been carefully planned. The slaves had used what we might call cells so that an individual slave would know of only a very few others who were part of the plot. They employed talking drums which had been widely used among the Asantes, and their secret network of rebels extended all the way to New Orleans.

François Trépagnier, Manuel and Gilbert Andry, Mathurin, James Brown, Harry Kenner, Jean Noel Destrehan, Bernard Bernoudy, Gustave and Dominique – all these figures who appear in *The Lion's Teeth* are documented parties to the events of 1811, either as slaves or as white planters who quelled the revolt. Most prominent of my sources is Daniel Rasmussen's *American Uprising, The Untold Story of America's Largest Slave Revolt,* which I recommend highly.

I have been faithful to the facts as I know them, but with embellishment. For instance, I have portrayed Gilbert Andry as a twisted soul, when in fact I know nothing of his character except that he was a slave owner. I have created Annique, Charles Deslondes' love, and imbued her with heart and soul while all we really know is that Deslondes had a woman on a nearby plantation. I imagined Kook and Quamana with the ritual scarring practiced among the Asantes back in Africa though none of my sources mention that these two men were marked. In my mind's eye, they were.

Another liberty I took was imagining that Mathurin and Deslondes could read. There were a few slaves who could read, but I do not know that these two men could. I also imagined that Deslondes knew about and was inspired by the successful revolt in Haiti that had taken place only a few years earlier. The refugees, white and black, who poured into Louisiana would have talked about it and it is probable that Deslondes would have heard the cry *égalité, fraternité, liberté.*

My goal in this fictional account is to put us into the minds and hearts of Deslondes, Kook, and Quamana as they attempt a great rebellion. Of course this rebellion and every other in America failed, but these men were great heroes in a glorious bid for freedom.

Bonus Section:

The first three chapters from
Gretchen Craig's new novel, *Tansy*.

Tansy

Chapter One

For weeks, before she slept, Tansy Bouvier imagined herself dancing with an elegant, handsome man whose gaze promised love and forbidden pleasures — only to waken later in a tangle of sweaty sheets, shaken by dreams of laughing men and women whirling around her, herself in an over-lit circle, alone, isolated, and unwanted.

But this was not a dream. The dreaded moment was upon her, the moment she had prepared for all her life, and she must smile. Maman gave her elbow a pinch, a final warning to sparkle. Tansy raised her chin and followed her into the famous Blue Ribbon Ballroom.

Droplets of fear trickled down her spine as she fought both the dread and the foolish romanticizing of what was essentially an evening of business. A beginning, not an end, she whispered to herself. Time to forget girlhood dreams, time to forget Christophe Desmarais. This night, she entered the world of plaçage in which a woman's *raison d'être* was to please a man, a very wealthy man. In return, she gained everything — riches, security, status.

In spite of the fluttering in her stomach, she found herself captivated by the glamour of the ballroom. Gas lamps glowed like yellow moons between the French doors, and crystal teardrops in the chandeliers sparkled like ice in sunshine. And the music. Tansy's chest lifted at the power and fire of a full orchestra, strings and reeds and percussion propelling the dancers around the floor.

Maman chose a prominent, imminently visible position near the upper curve of the ball room to display Tansy and her charms. Tansy's task tonight was to make a splash, to outshine every other girl who'd entered the game earlier in the season. No, she thought. Not a game. Tonight, Tansy would meet her fate: luxury or destitution, security or whoredom.

What if none of the gentlemen wanted her? What if none of them even noticed her? What then?

"Smile," Maman hissed from the corner of her mouth.

"I am smiling," Tansy replied through wooden lips.

"That is not a smile. Look like you're glad to be here. Watch the dancers."

White men in stiff collars wove intricate steps and turns through the line of women, every one of whom wore a festive tignon over her hair. Tansy squinted her eyes so as to make the dancers and the chandeliers a blur of lights and swirling colors. Such a grand, beautiful sight, as if the most renowned ballroom in New Orleans were not the scene of business and barter.

She had imagined the men as leering and brash. Instead they seemed aloof and slightly bored. The young women, though, were as she expected. They wore masks with bright smiles and welcoming, deceiving eyes that promised gaiety and delight. She was meant to do the same.

"Loosen your grip on that fan," Maman whispered. "It is not a sword to be brandished at the enemy."

Tansy swallowed and opened the fan with cold, stiff fingers. She spied her friend Martine on the dance floor, vibrant in a red velvet gown. How splendid she looked in the red tignon wrapped in intricate folds around her head. She laughed, her eyes sparkling as her partner leaned in to speak into her ear. Martine had already been to several balls and had regaled Tansy with tales of handsome gentlemen who whispered love and promises as they twirled her around the ballroom. She was having a grand time waiting for the right protector to offer for her, but Martine had a boldness, a carelessness, Tansy could not match. And Martine had never been kissed by Christophe Desmarais.

Tansy glanced again at her own yellow silk, the neckline cut so deep she felt indecent. If Martine was a vibrant scarlet tanager, she felt herself to be a mere mockingbird masquerading as a canary. She touched her matching tignon, terrified it might slip on her head. "I'm too conspicuous in this dress," she whispered to her mother.

"Nonsense. No other girl here can wear yellow like you can."

A Creole gentleman, dark haired, dark eyed, no doubt very charming, bowed to Maman. "Madame Bouvier."

Tansy breathed out in relief. She might feel conspicuous, but at least she was not invisible. The gentleman was tall and handsome, his nose straight and long, his brow rather noble. For a moment, she let herself believe this handsome man would fall in love with her, and she with him, and they would dance and laugh and feel drunk with love, together, forever. She wanted to believe it.

Tansy's foolish moment passed. Maman knew every gentleman in New Orleans and the status of his bank account. If the suitor were wealthy enough, he would be encouraged.

After the merest glance at Tansy, the gentleman murmured something polite to Maman, who nodded her approval.

He bowed to Tansy. "May I have the honor of this dance, Mademoiselle?"

With a curious feeling of detachment, she accepted his arm and followed him onto the dance floor. It was only a dance. She liked to dance. She'd let the music carry her.

The gentleman wore an expertly tailored coat of deep maroon paired with gray satin knee breeches. He did look very fine, but more to the point, very prosperous. He smiled at her. "Lovely evening."

I mean you no harm she interpreted. *See how nicely I smile? See how I have not once gazed at your plunging neckline, eyeing the wares?*

"Yes," she managed to say. "Lovely weather."

The dance led them near the orchestra's platform. Tansy darted a glance at Christophe, sitting among the violinists. Oh God, he was watching her. Her stomach dropped and heat rushed to her face. For the rest of the dance, she focused a frozen gaze on her partner's ear, and if he said anything else, she did not note it.

At the end of the set, the gentleman returned her to Maman, tossed a bow at her and went in search of more pleasing company. Maman scowled. "If you don't stop acting like a dry stick, I will take you home this instant."

Like the puppet she felt herself to be, she loosened her shoulders, unclenched her teeth, and obeyed. No dry sticks allowed. She would be a willow branch, graceful, pliable. Yes, that was her. Pliant Tansy Marie Bouvier, a willow to be bent to fit her destiny.

Tansy had a moment to collect herself as another Creole gentleman bent over Maman's hand and made the customary flattering remarks. He seemed pleasant, not inclined to devour young women at their first balls. He smiled. No, no fangs, no sharpened canines.

"Monsieur Valcourt, my daughter, Tansy Marie."

He was of medium height, medium build, medium dark hair and medium brown eyes. Not handsome, not ugly. Maman raised an eyebrow. Such a wealth of information in that eyebrow: this man is rich, this man is a catch, and if you know what's good for you, you'll make him fall in love with you.

"Mademoiselle, will you dance?"

Squaring her shoulders, she followed him onto the dance floor.

Tansy's resolve to ignore Christophe faltered and her eyes found him again. His focus was on the music, his brow creased in concentration. She knew men didn't set so much store in a kiss as women, but she would never forget it. She gave herself a mental shake. It was because of that kiss that her mother had dragged her here, two weeks before her seventeenth birthday, to ensure they both understood that Christophe, a mere fiddler, could not afford a beautiful canary like Tansy Marie Bouvier.

Monsieur Valcourt's attention seemed to be on the music, his gaze primarily directed over her shoulder as he moved her through the steps. He danced well. She liked the fact that he didn't try to charm her, nor did he seem to expect her to dazzle him.

They joined hands as they moved into a turn. Her cold fingers warmed in his palm, and his assumption of connection, of ease in their touch loosened her reserve. A comfortable man, this Monsieur Valcourt.

An older gentleman circled through the line to partner Tansy with a turn through the dance. He leered at her décolletage, yellow teeth on display, and he held his mouth slightly open with the tip of his tongue visible. The thought of his tobacco stained fingers in intimate contact with her skin sent a shiver of revulsion through her.

Or else, she remembered her mother's threat. Find a protector, or else face a life of penury, a few years in a brothel until your looks fade, and then what, eh?

The dance moved on and Monsieur Valcourt reappeared at her side. When he took her hand with no leer, no meaningful squeeze of her fingers, she breathed in freely for the first time all evening. The music ended. He bestowed on her an open, guileless smile that warmed his brown eyes.

Yes, she could live with this man. She didn't need to survey, and be surveyed by, a dozen or two other gentlemen. And if Maman was right, that her looks would assure her any man she chose, then she would as soon choose this one and have it done with. He seemed nice. They would likely have a family together. They would be happy enough.

She allowed herself one last glimpse of Christophe among the violinists. He met her gaze over his bow, and for a moment her vision tunneled so that all around him was hazy darkness, Christophe himself bathed in light. She closed her eyes and turned away.

Perhaps no woman could choose her own fate, but she would take control of what she could. She would be the placée of Monsieur Valere Valcourt.

Tansy opened her eyes and bestowed on Monsieur Valcourt her most dazzling smile.

Chapter Two

Five years later

Tansy danced with Annabelle's Monsieur Duval, he of the yellow teeth and dandruff-dusted shoulders. Her friend had skin two shades darker than her own and her wide nose reflected her African heritage, so of course Annabelle had not been able to attract the most desirable of protectors. Even so, she reported her patron kept her in comfort, never beat her, and came to her bed no more than once a week. He'd given her two wonderful children of whom he seemed fond, and she found her life reasonably happy. For that, Tansy smiled at him as he led her around the dance floor.

The new plaçeés-to-be danced all around her, dewy-eyed, round-chinned, and thrilled to be attended to by handsome, wealthy gentlemen. She spied one, however, who was as tense as Tansy had been at her first ball. And now, Tansy was at ease here in the Blue Ribbon ballroom, a woman more than twenty, a woman with a child.

The orchestra took a break. Monsieur Duval returned to Annabelle, and Tansy joined Christophe where he leaned against a column, the picture of languid ease. He dressed as all the musicians did, but on him the black jacket and white linen looked dangerous, the light in his roving black eyes distinctly carnal. She'd noticed more than one young woman eyeing him from behind their fans. But of course, as a man of color, however light, he was admitted here only as a musician.

Christophe handed her his glass of punch and nodded toward her dance partner. "You've made that old coot a happy man tonight."

"Maurice? He is an old coot, but a nice one." She finished his punch and handed him the glass, accidentally touching his fingers. Her breath hitched. They never touched, not since the night before her come-out in this very room. Trying to appear unfazed, she slowly fanned away the warmth in her face.

She eyed Christophe's scraped knuckles. "I see you've been brawling again."

He grinned. "Me? A shining example of virtue for all my students?"

She shook her head. "If they knew you were a brawler, they'd worship your very shadow."

"Don't tell, though. Their mamans and papas would not be well pleased. Have you noticed the Russians?"

"Is that what they are? I'd love to hear them speak."

He gestured for her to precede him. "Then allow me to introduce you."

"You've met them?"

"My legendary fame as a poker player has earned me an invitation to their table after the ball."

"I suppose you will show them no mercy."

With a wicked glint in his eye, he gave her a malicious smirk. "I will not."

They strolled toward the Russian delegation, Christophe's hands behind his back, a foot or more of space between them. She was well aware he took pains not to touch her. It was right that he do so. She belonged to Valere, after all.

"And where is your beloved paramour tonight?" he said.

Tansy stiffened at the slight curl in Christophe's lip. It was a game he played, trying to goad her into defending Valere, but she'd recently begun experimenting with goading remarks of her own.

"He's at the society ball across the alleyway, of course, with his cousins and friends. With the other *gentlemen*." She gave him a withering glance from head to toe to indicate how far he was from the status of gentleman.

Christophe chuckled. "Well done. You'll overcome your regrettable affliction yet."

She was indeed afflicted with an intransigent case of niceness, as Christophe called it. What he meant, she supposed, was that she was dull.

They split to walk around a cluster of people drinking punch. When they rejoined, Tansy fanned her face and looked about with an air of disinterest. "Valere courts a Miss Abigail, I believe."

"Miss Windsor? My fiddle and I played at her birthday ball in January. Pretty girl."

Tansy tilted her chin and looked down her nose at him.

"Forgive me. I have erred. I meant to report that the girl has buck teeth, a flat chest, and mousy hair."

"Indeed you should." Tansy drew her fan briskly through her left hand, in the age-old language of fans an indication that she detested him with all her heart.

Christophe threw his head back in a laugh. He nodded toward the arched doorway. "And here is the gentleman in question."

The slight ache of tension behind her eyes eased as Valere Valcourt leisurely made his way around the dancers, the hundreds of candles in the overhead chandeliers casting a gentle glow on his wavy brown hair. Descended from a disgraced French nobleman who'd been exiled to the wilds of Louisiana a century ago, Valere represented the quintessential Creole, privileged, entitled, at ease in his world.

Christophe slipped away. He had, as far as Tansy could remember, never actually been in Valere's presence.

Valere stopped to talk to Monsieur DuMaine, a man whom Tansy knew to be searching for his fourth placée, having tired of the others. Though he must be very rich indeed to have paid the penalties for breaking three contracts, he epitomized the most dangerous sort of protector in the world of plaçage. There could be no security in an alliance with a man of his reputation.

Martine, clad in her signature red, strolled past the two men, gently fluttering her fan in signal to Monsieur DuMaine. So Martine vied to be number four in this man's serial harem? Tansy did not like the idea of her friend allying herself with such a man. Tansy was no green girl, and the man was handsome, but really — didn't she understand he'd gone through three women in only five years?

Tansy watched Martine's little drama, worried at her friend's lack of judgment, but she was amused, too. Du Maine's eyes tracked Martine as she rolled her hips, touched a hand to her elaborate tignon to call attention to her slender neck, then made her way around the dancers toward the balcony. A scarlet tanager among wrens, she turned at the exit, raised her fan in her right hand to cover the lower part of her face, and flashed dark eyes at DuMaine. Mouth slightly open, he nodded vaguely toward Valere and strode away in pursuit. Tansy nearly laughed aloud at the man's haste.

Valere caught her eye across the room and smiled as he came to her. She put away her nagging jealousy over Miss Abigail Windsor. She had always known he would marry. He needed heirs, legitimate sons. His marriage didn't mean he would abandon her and their son. Valere's own father had raised his legitimate family with his very proper white wife, and yet had remained attached to the same placée for twenty years. She and Valere and Alain were a family now, regardless of when he married.

"Here you are," he said.

"Good evening, Valere." She smiled for him. She always smiled for him.

He stood at ease by her side, surveying the ball room, his glance falling on the group of large, bearish men in their rather rustic fashions.

"Do you see we have Russians here tonight?" she asked. "I would love to hear them speak, wouldn't you? And don't you suppose those heavy beards are hot? I don't imagine they're accustomed to our humidity."

"Russians, are they?"

And that was as much interest in Russians as she could elicit from him. So many other things she would like to talk about. Did the Society ladies dance until they glowed with perspiration? Had Valere danced all evening with Miss Abigail? But of course she could not speak of his other life.

"Shall we dance?" he said.

As Valere guided her around the dance floor, she yielded herself to the music, her mind adrift in the flowing colors of the violin, the oboe, the bassoon.

At the end of the number, Valere whispered in her ear. "Let's go home."

Tansy's lingering anxiety vanished. At least for tonight, Valere desired her, not the pale-faced Abigail Windsor.

Tansy reached for the blanket and pulled it over Valere's bare chest. In an hour or two, he'd get up to dress, then he'd leave her for his townhouse. In the morning, Alain would not even know his father had been there unless she told him. Valere took their son for granted, as he did so much in his life, but he was a good man.

Tansy lay a light kiss on his jaw and got up. She lit a candle, wrapped herself in her robe, and settled into the overstuffed chair with her book. This one was about Spaniards discovering the new world. How she would like to have been there when Columbus first made landfall, thinking he was in India. And found all those Indians! She stifled the laugh burbling up at the linguistic absurdity. She was just getting to the part where Cortés discovered the great city cut through with canals.

"Come back to bed and keep me warm." Valere's voice was muffled in his pillow. She blew out her candle and slid in beside him. "Cold feet! Woman, what have you been doing?"

She stuck one cold foot between his shins. "Reading. Did you know the Aztecs built a city very much like Venice? Canals through and around. And like New Orleans, the water table was so high, they practically lived in the marsh. I suppose it's even hotter in Mexico, though."

Valere tossed an arm over her belly. "Why is that?" he mumbled.

She moved her head to see his face on the pillow, but it was too dark to decide if he were teasing her. She suspected he was not. "It is so very much further south, you see."

"Is it?" He shifted to get comfortable. "Go to sleep, Tansy."

Chapter Three

Tansy helped Alain tie his shoes, took his hand, and set out for the Academy. She tried to do all her errands early in the day when she was sure Valere still lay abed in his townhouse and so wouldn't call while she was out. Her first task this morning, to return Christophe's History of the Americas.

She and Alain climbed the schoolhouse steps. Too early for the students yet, morning breezes wafted cool air into Christophe's schoolroom. Alain dashed for the resident cat who allowed herself to be caught and petted.

Christophe raised his head and in that one unguarded moment, revealed a depth of pleasure at seeing her that flashed through her with far too much warmth. "Good morning," he said.

"Finished the book."

He reached for it with his large, capable hand. That hand had once pressed her body against his. She'd been trimming the jasmine vine that threatened to cover the French doors and he'd stepped into the courtyard. With a gleam in his eye, a glance over his shoulder to check her mother was out of sight, he'd pulled her under the green canopy.

"What are you doing?" she'd whispered.

He caught her in his arms and dared her with his eyes. She could have backed away, like a good girl. But she'd let him pull her close. Let him lean down, the smell of jasmine and Christophe's own scent filling her head. She sighed. He kissed her. His hand traced her backbone till it rested at her waist, and then he pulled her in to his body. When he touched her tongue with his own, her breath caught. When he parted her legs with his knee and deepened the kiss, she completely lost herself in him, in the searing heat of his hand through the back of her dress.

Then Maman had stepped into the courtyard and shrieked as if a tiger mauled her only child.

Tansy jumped back, guilty and ashamed. But Christophe, all the while Maman scolded and railed, ran his thumbnail up her spine and then cupped her bottom and squeezed.

The next night, Maman had presented her at the Blue Ribbon Ball.

Tansy swallowed. She had no business remembering that stolen moment. She belonged to Valere. She was a mother. And Christophe was a respected man, a teacher, a musician. And yes, a gambler who sometimes showed up with a bruise on his chin and a busted knuckle. The two of them were no longer love sick adolescents.

"What did you think of it?" he asked.

"Very sad, the Aztecs losing everything to the Spanish, and then they died from those dreadful plagues." Did Christophe allow himself to think of that kiss? She didn't, she really didn't. She was settled now, and one long-ago kiss didn't mean so very much anyway.

"Not a happy story, no."

"Now I want a book about plagues."

Christophe laughed. "Aren't you the morbid one? Alas, my library is sorely limited." He swiveled his chair and ran his finger along the books shelved behind him. "How about this one?"

She looked at the spine. "*Candide.* What's it about?"

"Where would be the fun if I told you?" Christophe held his arm out. "Alain, come show me your letters."

Alain abandoned the tabby cat and climbed into Christophe's lap. When Alain glanced at her, a secretive smile on his face, Tansy raised her brows in collusion.

He picked up a chalk and laboriously drew an A on Christophe's slate. With his forehead scrunched in concentration, his tongue between his lips, Tansy thought him the most intelligent, handsome boy in New Orleans. He'd practiced his letters for weeks now and was about to astound his friend by writing his entire name.

"ALAIN?" Christophe exclaimed. "You wrote your name! *Tres bien!*"

Christophe hugged him and turned him around on his lap so he could look him in the eye. "You, Alain, are a great scholar."

"*Merci.*" Alain slid off Christophe's lap to pursue the cat.

Tansy sat at a student table and opened *Candide*. Christophe had given her her first book, too. In her last month of pregnancy with Alain, she had lumbered across the Quarter with Maman to visit Christophe's mother. By chance, Christophe had dropped in, a book under his arm. She'd not exchanged a single word with him since that day under the jasmine, but there was no distance between them. They talked and laughed and drank his maman's punch. When he rose to leave, he handed Frankenstein, the Modern Prometheus to her and said, "Keep it." And so Tansy read her first book, staying up late into the night, frightened and fascinated.

Christophe came around his desk and sat on a corner to lean over her.

"This one is fiction."

"Is it a love story?"

When she glanced up, Christophe's eyes were on her. Sometimes he focused on her as if she were a puzzle he'd like to solve. Sometimes, like now, she felt he would lift her to her feet and take her across the desk. He wouldn't though. Christophe had never deliberately touched her since their first, their only kiss.

She couldn't meet his eyes when he forgot himself like that. It unsettled her, it hurt her. In another time, another place ... Well. She was spoken for. She was so very fortunate to have a kind, generous patron like Valere. And really, Christophe had no interest in her any more. Just now and then she let herself think he did.

Christophe removed himself to sit behind his desk again, and she breathed more easily. "Not a romance, not like you mean," he said. "But it's fun. It'll make you laugh."

"You don't need it for your students?"

"Those rascals? They're not ready for satire, the little brutes. We're reading a story about a boy and his dog at the moment."

"I want a dog!" Alain said.

"I thought you wanted a cat," Tansy said.

"Maman, I want a dog and a cat."

"We'll ask your father. Perhaps he will allow a kitten."

Alain engrossed himself in the chalk nubs he found on the desks. Christophe's lowered voice barely suppressed his impatience. "Why would Valcourt object to Alain having a pet? Surely that is of no interest to a man who is seldom in the house when Alain is awake?"

When Alain was awake? Tansy's face heated and her shoulders stiffened. She busied herself putting the book in her shopping bag. "He doesn't like surprises, that's all."

She yanked the drawstring on her bag and knotted it too tightly. Christophe thought she was a fool, a childish fool, for deferring to her patron. How could he think that of her when his own mother had been a placée at one time. And yet he made her feel she led a lamentable life. She did not need his disapproval. Maman supplied enough of that for a dozen daughters.

"Alain." She held her hand out. "It's time to go."

"Tansy." She turned toward Christophe, but she still did not look at him. "I beg your pardon."

Now she raised her eyes to his and saw only a mask, rather cold, certainly closed off. "It's nothing. *Adieu*, Christophe. I'll return your book next week."

Christophe sat, elbows on his desk, his eyes closed behind his steepled fingers. Regret scorched him. He'd upset her, again. Her visits every week to borrow a book were too important to him to risk frightening her off, and he'd hurt her. When would he learn to keep his mouth shut? He should know better than to even mention Valcourt. She almost never did.

He rubbed his face. This was an old hurt. He simply had to accept the life she'd chosen. No, that wasn't right, he thought, the bitterness edging back into his mind. She had not chosen. Her mother had done that for her. Tansy had been too young, too immersed in the plaçage culture to see other possibilities for herself.

Estelle had molded her daughter into what every white man seemed to want, a biddable woman. Christophe remembered that day at the lake when they were children. His mother and Tansy's had taken them for an outing and he and Tansy had run wild, darting in and out among the tall pines, shrieking and shouting with abandon. That Tansy had been free and bold and unafraid. She had been herself.

But Estelle suppressed all that joy and used Tansy's inherent sweetness to turn her into a nice girl, a biddable girl. Except that one afternoon when he'd caught her under the jasmine vines and kissed her. Tansy had not been sweet or biddable then. She had seized that moment, seized him in a kiss that seared him to his toes.

Christophe ran a hand through his hair. Was she that hot when Valere took her to bed? He shook his head. He had no business thinking of that. Even if Estelle's steady hand propelled her, Tansy had entered into this life with her eyes open.

What added to the bitterness, though, was that he could have supported her from the time he was twenty, a year or so after she'd been taken to the Blue Ribbon. He had already begun investing his poker winnings by then and he'd quickly become a man of property with a growing bank account. He'd never be as rich as Valcourt, but he could keep her and Alain in comfort with his pay as a musician, his salary as a teacher, and his income from the houses he owned in the Vieux Carré.

He squeezed his eyes shut. If he'd only had a little more time, been a little older when Estelle sealed Tansy's fate.

He opened his eyes to stare across the room, trying to find the resignation that sustained him. When he'd met her at his mother's that day, her belly full and round, it had been nearly two years since he'd been in the same room with her. Tansy had been radiant. But weren't all women in her condition radiant? Or had she glowed with love for her protector? He hadn't known. And now? She had her fine clothes, her own cottage, a generous allowance. All she need do in return was pretend to adore some fatuous rich man who deluded himself he could buy affection. The muscles in Christophe's jaw bunched. Valere Valcourt was empty, vain, and idle, yet he possessed Tansy Marie Bouvier.

Did she live a lie, pretending to love that ass? Or had she actually developed an affection for him? Christophe hadn't made it out, and it gnawed at him.

The thunder of feet in the hallway announced his pupils had arrived, ready to have their heads stuffed with numbers and letters and facts. He breathed in deeply. When the rascals stormed into the room, he welcomed them with a smile he didn't feel.

~ ~ ~

You have been reading the first three chapters of Gretchen Craig's novel, Tansy. Available on Amazon in paperback and Kindle.

ABOUT THE AUTHOR

Gretchen Craig's award-winning novels, rich in memorable characters and historical detail, are profiled on her website at **www.gretchencraig.com**.

Further details are available at her Amazon Author Page at **amazon.com/author/gretchencraig**. Gretchen also invites you to visit her blog at **glcraig.wordpress.com**.